To Jerry, Jamie, and Shanna

MORNINGS IN LONDON

MORNINGS IN LONDON

A Francis Bacon Mystery

JANICE LAW

MYSTERIOUSPRESS.COM

OPEN ROAD

INTEGRATED MEDIA

NEW YORK

Copyright © 2017 by Janice Law

Cover design by Mauricio Díaz

978-1-5040-4501-8

Published in 2017 by MysteriousPress.com/Open Road Integrated Media, Inc.
180 Maiden Lane
New York, NY 10038
www.mysteriouspress.com
www.openroadmedia.com

MORNINGS IN LONDON

CHAPTER 1

Horses' hooves in the dawn—*my father's third-rate string heading off for the morning gallops.* That was my first thought, before I woke up enough to realize that my old life was mercifully long gone. I was grown up and far from Ireland and my father and all attendant miseries. No, even with my eyes still shut, I knew that I was a coming designer in London, my favorite place, and that any minute, I would hear Nan rattling in our small kitchen. She'd be filling the kettle and starting a rasher of bacon—if we were flush—and a couple of boiled eggs—if we were not.

Breakfast with Nan is almost the best possible start to a morning, and I opened my eyes, expecting my London bedroom with sketches pinned up on the walls and my drawing equipment strewn about, but . . .

No! I wasn't in Ireland, but I wasn't in London, either. I was in a big four-poster with a moth-eaten canopy, and the handsome haunch beside me under the blanket belonged not to Maurice, my Aussie lover, but to—oh, yes, now it all came back to me—the agreeable footman who had looked so handsome in his knee breeches. Pity they ever went out of style. I'd given him a wink as he served the soup and met him at the kitchen garden while the rest of the company played charades.

Footmen and charades and horsey guests off for a morning ride meant I was in the country; that was bad. I hate the country. The fresh air tortures my asthma and bores lengthen the days with charades and gardening and sport. I was trapped in a genuine country house with only Jenkins, the agreeable footman, as consolation.

Why was I so far from my native habitat, Soho, Piccadilly, and Hyde Park Corner? *Good question, Francis!* I fought off the aftereffects of a convivial evening to remember. I was here for my cousin Poppy, who is a favorite even though she was a deb and belongs to a country house set. I'm normally in a different set altogether, but I'm fond of my cousin, who has been promoting my interests lately, pointing out folks who might patronize Avant Design.

She's had me going to parties, infantile but with drinks flowing, where she'll say, "He's filthy rich, Francis, you must meet him," or "I've told her you're an artist and a genius and that she simply must have one of your rugs." Thanks to Poppy, whose talents are currently wasted on costume parties and scavenger hunts, some of her fancy friends have been supporting the arts. And speaking well of me, too, I reckon, because just recently Nan came home with a copy of *Connoisseur* and said, "Look here, dear boy, you're famous." Avant Design was splashed over two pages that showed my chairs, Bauhaus and Le Corbusier adaptations via a clever East End workshop. "Of course it's uncomfortable,"

I heard Nan say one day, "you're buying a piece of art." My nan has taken to sales like nobody's business. The magazine also featured my rugs, lovely if I do say so myself, with the tasteful color combinations I learned in Paris applied to avant-garde German geometrics.

All in all, wonderful for business, and a day after the issue hit the stands, Poppy paid me a visit. She swept in, greeted Nan, and without even a knock, opened the studio door. My cousin was dressed to the nines, looking quite ravishing and burbling with enthusiasm. She kissed me not once but twice, scolded me for not having the *Connoisseur* issue more prominent in the showroom, then grabbed my arm. "Someone you've simply got to meet," she said, adding sotto voce. "I'm quite mad about him, so be extra nice."

I put the caps on my colored inks and set aside a design for some drapes to match a rug already commissioned, finished, and, better yet, paid for. The fortunes of Avant Design were looking up. Out in the showroom, Nan was kitted out in one of her dark lady's companion's dresses and doing a good imitation of an all-knowing gallery attendant. My old nanny has many talents.

She was pointing out the innovative construction of a metal frame chair with a leather seat and back, genuinely new here in London, if clearly inspired by Continental designs. An elegant chap with a wave in his hair and a Savile Row suit was posed with his head tipped to one side, the better to take in the beauties of the piece. I was anticipating a sale with the possibility of a celebratory dinner with Nan and Poppy when he turned around. Oh, oh, trouble. Big trouble.

His name was Freddie. I knew him in a number of senses, and I knew his reputation, too, which was not only bad but dishonorable. A gentleman can withstand *bad*, but *dishonorable* is another matter, and both is a real obstacle. I was uncertain how to greet him, but he solved the problem with a blandly supercilious look. Perhaps I really had slipped his mind or perhaps designers were a step down from footmen.

"Freddie!" A trill in Poppy's voice and another deeper note that alarmed me. I did hope she wasn't serious about this one. "You must meet Francis, my oh-so-clever cousin. Descended, he likes to think, from the more famous Bacon, but not more famous for long."

That was Poppy all over. She could set my teeth on edge, but her heart was in the right place.

"Francis, this is Freddie Bosworth, and he's just right for a rug! And maybe a chair!"

Freddie looked less than enthusiastic. Too bad for him. I'd seen Poppy at work before.

"Really, Freddie," she added, "your flat is too boring for words."

We shook hands while Poppy fluttered and Nan adjusted the sample chair just so and gave our visitor an appraising look. In these troubled times, when credit can only be extended with the greatest of care, Nan has a good eye for who has money and, even more important, for who is likely to part with it.

"Unusual," was Freddie's judicious opinion.

"Exactly what you need," said Poppy. "But a rug first. Now, this"—she pointed to a beige carpet with interlocking circles of bronze and maroon—"is exactly the thing for your bedroom, but in blues. You can do it in blues, can't you, Francis?"

"Can do and have done." I fetched my sample book and went on about color families and current trends, all the while keeping an eye on Poppy and Freddie. She's a charmer with curly chestnut hair and greenish eyes, petite and graceful, but, as I remember from childhood, tough and up for just about anything.

She's a good rider, golfer, and tennis player—all the sporty things I'm bad at—and almost totally unspoiled by education. Just the same, we hit it off right from the start, and she was kind to me many times when I was unhappy as a boy. Now I could see that she was smitten, all right. What was the point of breaking hearts her whole deb year only to fall for a slimy item like Freddie Bosworth?

Let me be fair. Freddie was six feet of well-aligned bone and muscle with jet-black hair and blue eyes, a fine jaw and a broad forehead, altogether a tempting item if you could overlook his bullying arrogance. I'd known his ilk during my brief but dismal public school incarceration, and my experience has been that his type doesn't improve with age. But was that Freddie's case? Was the leopard about to change his spots, give up guardsmen in the Hyde Park bushes, and become fiancé, husband, paterfamilias? I didn't think so. I charged him a bit more than usual and didn't start his rug until Nan booked the deposit.

Poppy stopped by a week later to approve the design. She perched on the edge of my drawing table and studied the sketch. "This is perfect. If the colors are true."

I pointed to the bits of wool attached to the display board. "They are always a little different—colored inks are not the same as the dyes for wool. And remember, lighting in the room makes a difference, too. The rug will look different in artificial light and will change even during the day."

"Freddie's bedroom has a big north window," she said, giving me a look to let me know she was well acquainted with Freddie's sleeping arrangements.

"Perfect," I said. "North light is the truest light."

"Go ahead then. I'll work on him for a chair, too. His flat is a good size but quite old-fashioned."

"No appeal in nostalgic charm?"

"My thought is a complete renovation," she said briskly. "Top to bottom and all mod cons."

"You're serious about him, Poppy."

"I'm crazy about him."

I sat down in my drafting chair. "Oh, Poppy!"

She put her chin in the air, preparing to be stubborn, heroic, bullheaded. "What's the matter?"

"He's Lord Byron without the talent. *Mad, bad, and dangerous to know.*"

Poppy turned on her elegant heels and pretended to examine one of my sketches. "You're quoting, Francis. It's a bad, show-offy habit."

"I'm serious, Poppy. Think twice about Freddie. He's no gentleman."

"As if that ever mattered to you. As I recall, you've had some swains who were rather rough around the edges. Freddie's fun and he's interesting; I'm sick of bores who want to marry my money."

"The perils of being a beautiful deb. What does Freddie want?"

"Freddie's after my body, which is certainly refreshing. Plus he has his own money."

"He's delightful, though as for money . . ." Blackmail was actually the nicest of the Freddie Bosworth rumors, but I bit my tongue. For all her frivolity, Poppy will defend a friend to her last breath. I'd benefited from that sterling trait more than once.

"He has enemies, you know." She was earnest now. "He's warned me. People who don't approve of his politics."

"Which are?"

"Order and Christianity, of course." She spoke brightly, her moment of seriousness fled. "He quite worships Mussolini."

"I'm disappointed in you, Pops. It's much more fashionable to admire Stalin and the Reds."

"Left or Right, they're both mad. I hate politics," she said with the sudden passion that was Poppy all over. Brittle society chat hides her real feelings, which I'm beginning to think may frighten her. "We had the hunger marchers pass our back garden. Who's doing anything for them? I'll tell you who, only Mosley. He's the only one with a plan."

"At the moment, he's running a group of Blackshirts who beat up Jews in the East End." I knew that because some of my suppliers were German Jews fresh out of the Reich. Farsighted men, experienced in the carpet and furniture trades, who were now running small workshops in Hackney.

"Freddie says—" Poppy began, then stopped, perhaps sensing

that I had no interest in what Freddie thought. *In the future, Francis, keep your ears open and your mouth shut.*

She hopped off the table and pulled on her gloves. "Rush the order, won't you, dear? Freddie's birthday's coming up, and I've found the most divine vase imaginable, a perfect blue to match his eyes."

With that, she swanned off, and I heard nothing more from her for several weeks—although I saw an announcement of her engagement in the *Times*. The rug came in, was delivered, was— hurrah—paid for by a check that proved good. Then I got an invitation, a formal invitation in a formal envelope from people I'd never heard of, to a weekend party in Sussex. This was immediately followed by a note from my cousin, a hasty scribble unlike her usual hand and quite without her bantering tone and promises of rich clients:

Francis,

Accept the invitation from the Larkins. I'm in a desperate state and need you beside me. Please don't let me down.

Poppy

What else could I do? Nan resurrected my evening clothes and insisted on a tweed jacket and plus fours for day.

Talk about a costume party!

"Remember you were raised to be a country gentleman," Nan said, and she would brook no dissent. My old nanny judges not, except in matters of dress and manners that reflect badly on my upbringing, which was mostly, and certainly most significantly, conducted by her. I was allowed to draw the line at an ascot. With my country house kit perfect, I set off from Victoria to help my cousin in her hour of need.

What did I find when I arrived? The flowing tears of some ghastly personal catastrophe? No, just a rather grand and very old country seat, complete with tenant farms and all the usual asthma-provoking livestock. I was met at the front door by the butler, heavy and white-haired, with enough gravitas for a cabinet minister. He told me that Miss Penelope was out driving with Mr. Freddie in the pony cart. Cross off one worry: If Pops had horse and whip in hand, Freddie would do well to keep in line.

In the meantime, entertainment was laid on for me. There were gardens to see, still at their pollen peak, and acres of ancestor portraits, with not even a Lely among them. There were shrubberies, too, crowded with rhododendrons, which I might have reconnoitered had I spotted the agreeable footman a bit earlier. There were meandering walks and a pond, a little banqueting house, and, just beyond the stables, roughly two and a half stories' worth of an early Norman ruin. My host, Major Larkin, regretted that this crumbling pile was set so close to the modern buildings; farther on amid the trees, it would have created "a charming prospect." I was thankful it was no farther. I'd already had the full inspection tour, because the lord of this pretty manor, educated at Sandhurst and wounded at Ypres, was in love with his estate. I never have luck with military types.

The major knew the age and provenance of everything, from the crypt in the oldest wing to the trophy spears in the billiards room to the big copper boilers in the kitchen, and he was eager for an audience and tireless as a guide. Having learned from Poppy that I was a designer, Magnus Larkin decided that I must be interested in architecture and furnishings, especially his. While other guests snoozed in their rooms or dozed in the library, I was escorted from top to bottom and assailed along the way by the dust of the centuries.

By dinnertime, only family feeling stood between me and the fast train back to London. I said as much to Poppy, who seemed as sprightly as ever when she finally appeared. Despite the desperation of her note, she had not sought me out when she returned from her drive. No, indeed, I met her in the corridor shortly before the dinner gong. She barely paused on her way to the stair, just touched my arm, and said, "Francis, you've come!"

I was feeling cranky. "For what reason is the question."

A pause, a beat. "You think I've gotten you here on false pretenses," she said. "But you'll see."

Then she tripped down the stair and into the salon, where she took Freddie's arm for the ceremonial procession to the dining room. As a usefully unattached male, I was paired up with the major's cousin, an elderly dame with a cloud of face powder and a roguish eye. She entertained me with accounts of parties past and of earlier generations of Larkins, a family history that made me think Freddie would fit right in.

He was up toward the head of the table, opposite Poppy, who I observed was not as merry as usual. She avoided eye contact with me and kept giving Freddie sharp, observant glances, while he made himself agreeable to Mrs. Larkin, a large woman with a Roman nose and an air of command.

"Of course, Eveline has the money," my dinner companion said, observing my interest. She nodded sagely. "She fancies herself an influence, don't you know."

I didn't. "Influence?"

"Politics." The old dame nodded her head. "The crowd of New Party people. I think only good taste keeps them from the BUF."

"Mosley's fascists?"

"The same. My father was an admiral. I disapprove of men wearing military dress unless they've taken the king's shilling."

I had to agree. I'd seen enough of uniformed men, except perhaps for footmen. I couldn't help giving one of them the eye.

With a wicked giggle, the old lady leaned over to whisper in my ear. "That's Jenkins. Used to be a dozen like him for every table. Before the war, they employed a footman for each guest. Imagine."

I could. I realized that I had been lucky to be seated below the salt and beside one of the more entertaining guests. The middle of the table held two gentlemen with Conservative Party connections who were talking shop, while from the head of the table, the major lectured their bright-eyed wives on church brasses, specifically those in the ancient church that was part of his fief. Doubtless, I'd see that tomorrow.

There was also the Larkins' younger daughter, a sallow-faced miss with her mother's nose and her father's volubility, flirting across the table with a young man from the Italian embassy. I was surprised to see him. I'd expected enthusiasm for the Mussolini regime to wane after the poison gas attacks in Eritrea, but the Larkins and their guests had strong stomachs, as conversation with the men of the party later confirmed. They were all for landed wealth, the Church of England, the empire, and old moral standards. Freddie met my eye at that and gave a little smirk. Careless of him, if he was serious about marrying Poppy, but then he'd been heavy on the wine all during dinner, and he was already deep into the scotch. Something on his mind or just a permanent thirst?

I couldn't begin to guess, and I didn't really care, because Poppy clearly had the situation in hand. My desire for an early night required enthusiasm for a visit to the family church the next day. "Early Norman crypt," the major said, "and some very interesting Jacobean furnishings."

"Fascinating," I said and set off to find the handsome footman Jenkins.

The same Jenkins was now rolling out of bed and collecting his clothes. He eased open the door with practiced care and disappeared into the corridor. I checked my watch. It was six fifteen. I had a full day of country delights ahead of me.

CHAPTER 2

I grabbed the bathroom before the other guests lined up. The manor house had been updated with indoor plumbing around the turn of the century, an improvement that caused the major both pride and regret. His father and grandfather had been "forward looking" but not always as "respectful of the fabric" as the present owner.

"A time capsule," he said. "One of the great resources of England. A great house carries the nation's history."

I could but nod. At the time, we were admiring the first indoor convenience, centrally located off the entrance hall, with a marble seat, handsome tile work, and the faint but penetrating odor of ancient drains. The upstairs facilities were more comfortable if less historic. Washed and ready for the day, I stepped into the hallway to see Signor Rinaldi. Wearing a fine cashmere dressing gown and carrying his toiletry bag, he was just leaving Freddie's room.

I knew it was Freddie's, because we had heard someone pass my door in the night, and Jenkins, who clearly knew every creak of the stair and every board in the corridor, said, "That's Mr.

Freddie. He staggers when he's drunk," before we heard the door opposite mine close.

"Morning," I said.

When he saw me, Signor Rinaldi stuck his free hand into his pocket and looked ready to sink through the floor, but he recovered with a big smile, revealing quite splendid teeth. "Signor Freddie is early awake."

"Out riding, I expect. With his fiancée."

"The beautiful Miss Penelope, of course! My mistake!" He clapped a theatrical hand to his forehead and said something in rapid Italian, before adding, "I was returning a book he so kindly lent me." With this, Rinaldi gave a little bow and slipped into the bathroom, locking the door behind him.

Well, well. Shared reading material? The latest novel out of Rome in the original Italian? I didn't think so. Poor Poppy! The leopard was still a spotted cat, and the sooner she dropped Freddie, the better. I thought I should tell her that and then I thought I should keep my mouth shut. I still hadn't decided when the riders returned with a bustle in the front hall.

"Wait, Poppy!" Freddie's voice was full of suppressed agitation.

My cousin's voice rose an octave above. "Only my friends call me Poppy!"

"You don't understand my situation—"

"I understand it perfectly now! I should have listened—" Then a door slammed.

I stepped into the hallway. The two of them were closeted in the library, where they felt free to shout. "I could just kill you," I heard Poppy scream.

Not a bad idea, but she would have been better to keep her voice down, for the other riding ladies were distressed, and their consorts, embarrassed. Shouting and threats of what Nan's favorite crime columns call "grievous bodily harm" are bad form at country house parties. We had a few moments of paralyzed awkwardness before Freddie banged the door against the major's prized paneling and clattered upstairs in his riding boots.

Signaling for the others to wait, I entered the library and closed the door softly behind me. I guessed that I'd been invited because Poppy had suspected the lay of the land, now confirmed. She was standing at the far end of the handsome room, all fine mahogany cabinetry and leather-bound volumes. I joined her at one of the long windows, and we did not speak for several minutes.

"You knew," she said finally. "You knew all about him. I blame you for this."

That was going too far even from the brokenhearted. Although I loathe *I told you so*, I said, "I did try to warn you. I told you he was a terrible man and to stay clear of him."

"But you weren't convincing, Francis." Poppy attempted her usual arch manner despite her trembling lip. "You weren't convincing at all."

I put my arm around her. "You were in love."

"Love," she said bitterly. "Love is supposedly kind, but I could cut his throat. Now I'm not sure I know what love is."

I drew Poppy close to me and stroked her hair. I wasn't a big expert on love, either, though I'm pretty knowledgeable about lust, its disreputable sibling. Maybe I told her that. I think I did, because she wiped her eyes and used her handkerchief.

"Can we go now? I'll be a gentleman and escort you back to London."

Poppy stiffened immediately. "Leave a house party because of Freddie? I'm not the one sneaking around with that slimy consul or attaché or whatever the hell he is. Let Freddie crawl back to London."

I saw her point, but I wasn't going to accompany her grieving ex-fiancé back to civilization. "You're condemning me to church brasses and Jacobean oak and an early Norman crypt."

"Do you good, Francis. Exert yourself and see if you can't convince Major Larkin to add a modern rug to his collection. Oh, and perhaps you'll return this to Freddie." She twisted a handsome sapphire-and-diamond ring from her finger and dropped it into my hand. Then she put her chin in the air and walked out.

The end of Poppy's engagement undeniably enlivened the party. Everyone had an opinion on the breakup, and everyone was eager to talk about it, with the exception of the major, whose head remained in the architectural clouds. Our visit to the small Norman church actually provided a welcome break, and what was even more welcome was learning on our return that Freddie had been driven to the London train. Good riddance!

When I'd returned the ring, he'd struck me as angry rather than sad, confirming Poppy's narrow escape. Later, I supported my cousin during an unpleasant lunch. The other guests were uncertain where to look or what to say, but, if anything, Poppy was overly bright, the deb's way of defying fate and showing the flag. She insisted on my giving an account of the Norman church, an account continually amplified and corrected by the major. This got us through the soup and fish and most of the way through the roast before an uncomfortable silence fell.

Mrs. Larkin took up the running with remarks on the Conservatives' prospects that led by devious paths to the mysterious Wallis Simpson. The major's wife claimed to have good intelligence about this lady, and I pricked up my ears, for if there is one thing Nan enjoys more than good crime coverage, it's royal gossip.

"She was with him at Ascot," said Peter Tollman. The older of the Conservative gents was tall and very conscious of his silver hair and fine profile. He'd been in various government posts and assisted the major with his investments.

"That's public knowledge." Mrs. Larkin leaned forward confidentially. "I can tell you that they were together on the Riviera."

"Surely not on the royal yacht!" This from Daphne Grove, who my father would have called a "horsey lady." She had a strong face, burned red from sun and wind; curled blond hair; and large, strong hands. Top to toe, she suggested established money.

"My dear! Certainly not. On a wealthy friend's. Some Greek magnate, I think, a man with connections. Here and there." She sniffed and added, "Including some that wouldn't bear examination, I should think."

"Not much danger for the king, though, seeing the lady is married," said Basil Grove. Younger than Tollman, robust, complacent, and shrewd, he supplied furniture to the big department stores. "Lord spare us from Americans."

"Mrs. Simpson is married in name only," observed Mrs. Larkin.

"And supposedly, she knows the way to the divorce court,"

Lea Tollman added in a high, fluting voice. "This is husband two—or is it three?" She twitched her dark, plucked eyebrows and smirked.

Everyone laughed at this.

"I shouldn't worry about the lady from Baltimore," said Peter. "A divorced woman as royal consort! The British public wouldn't stand for it. I tell you, the British public is sound. Not to mention the C of E."

Opinion was uniform on this, although Poppy did mention that the Church of England might look to its founder on the matter.

The ensuing laughter led the major, stronger on history than tact, to observe that Henry VIII found beheading easier than divorce. This caused the party to remember the morning's scene and rather dampened conversation.

Soon afterward the pudding was finished, and we left the dining room, Poppy to retire to her room. I took a turn through the shrubbery on the forlorn hope of seeing Jenkins, then went to the library where I paged through a handsome edition of Shakespeare. My tenure in school was mercifully brief, but I love books and mean to be educated. I was deep in the tragedy of Richard II, who, like me, had a taste for handsome men, when Poppy came in, leaned on the back of my comfortable leather chair, and looked over my shoulder.

"Richard II. Wasn't he an early York or something?"

"The last Plantagenet. The play has some marvelous verse."

"You have surprising enthusiasms, Francis," she said before she raised my hopes by adding, "I need to get out."

"You're so right. You need London, a night at the theater, followed by a club with a jazz band and very strong cocktails."

"I'll settle for a walk," she said and took my arm.

Outside, Poppy immediately went quiet and stayed silent through a long walk down the grassy lanes that skirted the pastures and the tenant farms. We loitered long enough to miss tea, and the light had shifted to the west before we reached the field below the stables and the major's prized ruin. The track was quite steep there, the old Normans having selected what the military minds in my family would call "a defensible and dominating site." At the bottom of the track, some earlier Larkin landscaper had planted a grove of oaks, creating a nice prospect from the fields. We were passing through the shadows when Poppy drew in her breath and stopped.

"What's that?" The first thing she'd said for more than an hour.

I followed her glance to the base of the tower, spotted something dark sprawled awkwardly in the weeds, and felt uneasy. "Just a bundle of rags?" Though where would they have come from? "A sleeping vagrant?" Quite likely, I thought, I hoped, for though we were assured the worst of the depression was over, homeless wanderers and itinerate job seekers were still all too familiar.

"No. No, that's a good suit, that's—" She started forward with me a step behind. Then she gave a cry, and I grabbed her arm and held her back.

"Poppy, no!"

She stopped, shock making her biddable. I stepped around her. The man was lying facedown, but I recognized the fine pin-striped fabric, well-cut black hair, and expensive shoes. This was no vagrant.

I took a big breath and knelt down, but I knew before I put my hand on his shoulder—and even before I saw the red-and-black gash across his throat—that Freddie was dead. I took another breath and found my legs.

"Is he?" Poppy had edged closer.

"Don't look," I said. "Yes."

"Oh, God, this is my fault," she cried and burst into tears. "Was he hurt somehow?"

I nodded.

"What, what was it, Francis?"

She moved to step closer and I held up my hand. "He was attacked. His head and his throat. You don't want to see it."

She gave a great wail of pain and her legs folded. She pounded the grass with her fist as if she really had been crazy about Freddie, as if all her clever remarks and teasing and frivolity were just a mask, as if underneath she was someone who could threaten a lover and mourn his death like a madwoman. "I wanted him dead! I did! But I didn't mean it. Oh, Francis, if only I hadn't said anything! And now there he is."

"Poppy, get hold of yourself."

"But, Francis, it's my fault. It really, really is."

"You didn't kill him, did you?"

She sobbed and denied it.

"Well then, we have to get the police and you best be careful unless you want to be 'assisting with police inquiries.' This may be messy."

As soon as I spoke, I knew it would be. Freddie's death provided just the story ingredients my dear nan adored: a country house, society folk, a dodgy corpse, a grieving fiancée—regrettably, in this case, ex-fiancée. However desirable the morning's blowup had been for my cousin's future, it was not the best thing at the moment.

"There will be police." Her voice was flat.

"Yes."

"And press. There will be press, won't there, Francis?

"You can count on it."

"How I used to love being in the papers! All my deb year and ever since, too. What a fool I was! They'll have my pictures. Francis. Mugging for the camera and posing in silly costumes! Poor Freddie! It's not right that he'll be in with such nonsense, is it?"

She was unfocused by shock, and I gave her a shake. "Poppy, you must be careful. Say as little as possible. And don't read the papers."

"But we must find who did this to Freddie!" She wiped her eyes. "He could be irresistible, you know, Francis."

Actually, I did know that.

"He was awfully handsome."

"His undoing," I said and helped her up. Poppy was trembling; I didn't feel too solid myself. We staggered up the slope, past the stables and into the house. Fortunately, Jenkins met us at the door.

"Get Miss Penelope a drink, a stiff one, please, Jenkins. Somewhere quiet if you could."

"No one's in the morning room, sir."

I handed Poppy off to the footman and went to the salon.

Everyone was still gathered around the tea table, Mrs. Larkin presiding. When she saw me, she raised her head and stretched her wattled neck like an annoyed fowl. Missing tea was bad form.

"Major Larkin, might I speak with you privately? Something very urgent."

He was surprised, but I must have looked and sounded shocked. I stepped back into the hallway and led him away from the door. "You must call the police," I said quietly.

"The police? Whatever's wrong? Not more of those damn hunger marchers?"

"No, far worse."

I told him what we'd found and watched his eccentric duffer manner slide away. By the time I was finished, he was metaphorically standing atop the trenches, ready to order the advance.

"Your cousin?"

"In shock. I asked Jenkins to give her a drink. She's in the morning room."

"Right. I'll get my wife to—"

"Maybe I should look after Poppy," I said quickly. "There's no need to alarm the others yet."

When he hesitated, I added, "I could do with something stronger than tea, myself."

"Right. Steady on. I'll call the police. But take your cousin directly to her room. She won't want a lot of questions at the moment."

Nor later, either, but those could not be avoided after the local constabulary arrived, a contingent consisting of a man on a motorbike, the local doctor, and two husky constables in a battered police van. The major led them to the base of the tower, and as soon as they took in the situation, they used the house phone to summon reinforcements. An hour later, another car arrived, this one new, black, and official. Two men got out; the older, tall, stoop-shouldered, and dressed in a bulky tweed coat, was Alex Carstairs, a detective inspector from Hastings.

He had a long sallow face, small eyes in dark pouches, shadowed cheeks, and an air of terminal boredom. His fingers were stained brown from the cigarettes that he smoked compulsively. I never saw him except veiled in a bluish cloud, all the better to hide any expression in his narrowed eyes from witnesses, suspects, and villains.

As the discoverers of the corpse, Poppy and I came in for special attention. Of course, I described finding the body straightaway.

"Did you move the body?" he asked.

"Certainly not. I touched his shoulder, thinking maybe he was hurt not dead. And then I saw his throat and the blood on the grass."

"The body was lying quite close to the wall of the tower," he observed.

"That's right. Very close. Without the wound in his neck, I'd have figured he'd fallen," I said. Indeed, thinking about his position, I wondered how his assailant had managed at all.

"Was there a way up into the tower?" Inspector Carstairs asked.

"I don't know. When Major Larkin showed me around, we stayed on the ground."

The inspector puffed for a moment on his cigarette, then thanked me for my information. That was at dusk.

Once the van had carried Freddie away, the police commandeered the library. Inspector Carstairs cleared its large table and
set up shop with his assistant, a weedy-looking sergeant with a
bony face and a quick, alert manner. Carstairs worked his way
through the guests, collecting names and addresses, and trying,
as he put it to me on our second interview, to "get a picture of
the deceased and establish a time line of events."

The deliberate and cautious inspector did everything with an
absolute poker face and a neutral voice. On my second interview,
I tried to operate the same way, thinking over each answer. To lie
to the police is stupid. But to volunteer information unnecessarily is foolish.

"You say you went out at four forty-five p.m.?" Carstairs
began. We had, of course, established this at our first interview.

"Thereabouts," I said.

"That was"—here he consulted a note on his pad—"nearly
time for afternoon tea."

I nodded.

"Might that have been considered discourteous?"

"Not under the circumstances, I don't think. Poppy—Penelope—wanted to take a little walk. She'd been terribly upset."

"By breaking her engagement?"

"That's right."

"Although it was her decision?"

"One can decide something and still be upset."

"She was upset enough to threaten to kill him. Is that correct?"

I wondered which of our guests had added that tidbit. Maybe
all four of the riders, who seemed both horrified and thrilled by

events. "She and Freddie were having a row," I said. "The 'threat' was in a manner of speaking."

He checked his notes again. "Do you know what caused the breakup?"

I shrugged. "She discovered that Freddie was not the man she thought he was."

The inspector stared at me and waited. I said nothing. Ever since my Aussie lover started giving me painting lessons, I've been really looking at faces. Faces are very interesting to me as a subject, so I studied the inspector's while he waited for me to reveal that I knew all about Freddie's sexual habits, that I'd seen Signor Rinaldi coming out of his room, that Poppy had probably discovered the same relationship.

Eyes strike one first, but, for painting, the nose is also a key feature, dividing the face and setting its length. I'm finding it easy to get proportions wrong. The shape of the lips is tricky, too, since they are so mobile during speech. The inspector's were still at the moment, and I noticed his wide, almost squared-off mouth. Dentures, I guessed. An interesting line, broken now, as he asked, "Did you know Mr. Bosworth?"

Tricky ground for me when our sceptered isle remains in the Dark Ages regarding erotic variety. "He commissioned a rug from me. Poppy brought him around to my showroom, maybe six weeks ago. I have the exact date in my account book. In London."

I tried to look eager and helpful. Could I be released to London, how cooperative I could be! The inspector narrowed his eyes still more and consulted his notes again. "You returned the engagement ring to Mr. Bosworth."

I nodded.

"And spent the rest of the morning with Major Larkin?" He made that seem like a doubtful proposition. It was.

"The major knows the history of Larkin Manor. The ruined tower was built soon after the conquest, and the church he took me to see also dates from the Norman era. He found a lot to explain."

"You returned, when?"

"Time for lunch."

"And after?"

"Except for stretching my legs for a few minutes in the shrubbery, I spent the afternoon in the library. It has all the classic authors."

I don't think the inspector was a reader. He certainly didn't credit that I had spent the afternoon with Shakespeare.

"Who can confirm this?"

"Jenkins brought me a glass of beer. Otherwise, I did not see anyone."

"And your cousin, Miss Dinesmor? Did you see her during that time?"

"Not until late in the afternoon. She came down to the library around four thirty, and said she wanted to go for a walk."

"And you have no idea where she was before that?"

"I believe she came down from her room."

The inspector stared at me without speaking for a minute, then asked, "Can you describe what she was wearing?"

"A gray woolen skirt, a heather-colored sweater, and a Liberty print blouse. Walking clothes."

"And at lunch? How was your cousin dressed then?"

"A garnet-colored day dress and high heels."

The inspector closed his notebook. "That will be all for the moment," he said, but he looked dissatisfied, and conversation with the other guests revealed that except for Poppy and me, those two unsociable souls, everyone had an alibi. Of sorts. The two Conservative gents had spent the afternoon playing billiards with Rinaldi. The major had caught up on some accounts with the butler. Mrs. Grove and Mrs. Tollman had spent the afternoon in the latter's room, reading novels and summoning the staff every so often for assistance with a frock or a cup of tea or to do a bit of sewing.

Young Miss Larkin and her mother were engaged in preparing for an upcoming trip to Italy and making plans for extensive clothing purchases, while the elderly cousin alternately gave them advice and dozed in an armchair. Poppy had been seen at the stables immediately after lunch, but the head groom confirmed that she had walked back toward the house and that she was still wearing dress clothes, quite unsuitable for scrambling up Norman ruins.

As for yours truly, I had Jenkins and that welcome glass of beer to confirm my afternoon in the library, not much really, but several other alibis depended solely on the word of the manor's staff, too, so I was not surprised when we were shortly told that the house must be searched, including our rooms and our bags. Although the major frowned and said that the police were just doing their job, Mrs. Larkin was horrified, while the rest swore up and down that none of Freddie's friends could possibly be involved.

I reserved judgment on that. The chance that some tenant farmer in Sussex had known Freddie well enough to want to cut his throat seemed remote. And then Freddie had not been found off in the fields or along the road from the station. He had been found right below the stables. Where could he been going except back to the house? And for what reason?

Nonetheless, I went along with the proposition that we were all innocent as lambs, and when Poppy, whose nerves were all on edge, considered indignation, I put my hand on her shoulder and said, "Very best thing. Unless the search turns up some blood-soaked garment or lethal weapon, the police will have no reason to detain us. We'll be off to London in the morning!"

She sat down heavily on her bed and bit her lip. "There will surely be a Sunday service, Francis. No, no, we'll have to attend. Given the circumstances."

She seemed about to cry, and I had to admit that a too hasty departure suggested remorse if not guilt. "All right, afternoon, Poppy. Afternoon we're on the train to London. No more Norman architecture, no more horses, no more endless country afternoons!"

Just then, one of the constables knocked at the door and, with apologies, proceeded to rifle through Poppy's suitcases and the bureau drawers—she did, I noticed, have some deliciously elegant underwear, as well as a neat little box with a contraceptive device. But there was no bloodstained blouse or skirt, and even her laundry, set aside for the chambermaid, was spotless. Just the same, the constable lifted the mattress and checked under the small Oriental rug that stood by the bed. He looked behind the drapes and into the wastebasket and made sure that there was nothing hiding in the small writing desk. I was impressed.

My room also got the once-over. Same drill: suitcase, closet, laundry—my two suits and two shirts did not give him the same scope as he'd had with Poppy's wardrobe. Bedding, drapes, washstand. My books and sketching equipment got a curious look before he moved on to the next rooms. I would have liked to see what Signor Rinaldi's room held, but they must have come up empty there and in the other rooms, too. Shortly after 10 p.m., when we were finishing the buffet of cold roast and sandwiches that the cook had provided in lieu of a sit-down dinner, Inspector Carstairs came into the dining room, took a sandwich and a cup of tea, and said that we could leave in the morning but that we were to notify him if we traveled anywhere except to our legal residences.

CHAPTER 3

We attended Sunday morning service in the Larkins' damp and chilly Norman church. The vicar, never having met Freddie, prayed for his spotted soul with touching earnestness and mentioned his grieving friends with a straight face. Aside from Poppy, who sniffled throughout and thanked the vicar profusely, I could not see that anyone felt more than inconvenience, not even Signor Rinaldi, supposedly the cause of the broken engagement.

I kept a close eye on him, but the Italian seemed so untroubled that I began to doubt any relationship at all with Freddie. Maybe he'd told the truth. Maybe he had returned something to Freddie's room that morning and maybe Poppy had jumped to the right conclusion on flawed evidence.

As for the others, the major and his lady focused on the service, prudent when scandal had visited their house. I could see that they trusted public piety to show them unimpeachable. The Tollmans and the Groves, on the other hand, were restless in their pews. They checked their watches and stared at the ceiling and suggested with every pose and gesture that none of this had anything to do with them. So I wasn't surprised that when Basil Grove thanked the vicar afterward, he added, "Of course, I hardly knew the man. I'm not sure we'd met him before this weekend, had we, dear?" Or that she answered, "Well, unless you met him in the City. I think he moved in different circles altogether." That, at least, was true, if nothing else.

When we got back, the police were busy on and around the tower and in the grove of trees and the adjacent pasture. The constables had roped off the crucial area. Some were searching through the stonework and the rubble of the tower; others were walking slowly, heads down, across the grass.

Peter Tollman appeared on the terrace with a cigar. "What the hell are they about?"

"I expect they are looking for the murder weapon."

"Fat chance they'll find it," he said, and I looked at him. The usual line, now that we were free to go, was that the police would soon sort out the matter.

I shrugged. Privately, I agreed that the weapon that had opened Freddie's throat was unlikely to be found. The manor had plenty of hiding places, and the fields beyond offered more.

"You can't think they'll find anything," Tollman persisted.

"Needle in a haystack," I said, "even here."

"Here? You can't be serious. Chap will have taken it with him if he's a transient of some sort."

"Why would such a person have killed Freddie?"

"He had money on him," Tollman said, and then he coughed as if flustered that he'd given something away. "That's right. You'd already gone up. We had a few hands the other night, and Freddie won some money at cards."

"Do you know for sure he was robbed?" I very much regretted not checking Freddie's pockets.

"No other reason I can see, and if he was robbed, whoever did it will be far away by now. Headed for the Continent I shouldn't wonder."

I doubted that desperate rural poverty would operate that way, but I said nothing. Tollman took a deep drag on his cigar then turned to me. "Did you know him?"

"Freddie? Not really. He bought a rug from me."

Tollman sniffed. "Strange duck. Really more Lea's friend than mine." He threw the butt of his cigar onto the drive and walked off to see about his car.

The plan for the day was that Poppy and I were to stay for lunch with the major, his wife, and her superannuated cousin. The Groves were taking a noon train, and the Tollmans were to drive back with Signor Rinaldi. I saw him tipping my agreeable friend, Jenkins, as I stepped into the hallway with my bag. "A moment, Signor Bacon, if you please."

I waited. Jenkins took my bag, pocketed my tip, and gave me a wink. Did Rinaldi notice? Although the Italian had been standoffish the whole weekend, clearly too important for a small fish like me, he was suddenly friendly, even confidential. "Such a sad ending to the Larkins' charming party," he said.

I agreed with that.

"And unfortunate that you and I have had so little time to talk."

I expressed my regret with a straight face and added, "Under the circumstances—"

"The distress of your fair cousin! Most certainly. I wonder, Signor Bacon, was the rupture a complete surprise?"

"What do you mean, Signor Rinaldi?"

"I did not get the impression that you knew the Larkins well. Nor the other guests, either. Perhaps your cousin arranged your invitation?"

I didn't see what business that was of his, but I was interested in his attitude. "How perceptive you are. You're right, Poppy got me invited; she was maybe having second thoughts."

Signor Rinaldi nodded vigorously and seemed relieved in some way, as if there had previously been something vaguely sinister about my presence. "To have a relative beside her, a young man of the world—an inestimable benefit! She is a fortunate young lady."

I am not often endorsed so glowingly, and I was tempted to mention some of the fine products of Avant Design. But I was raised to be a gentleman, a drawback for someone hustling for trade. "She is most unhappy at the moment," I said and moved toward the stairs.

"Of course, you must escort the lovely Miss Dinesmor. But Freddie Bosworth, did you know him well?"

The question of the morning! "I sold him a rug," I said.

Rinaldi bit his lip. I could see he was dissatisfied, but all he said was, "You would have found him fascinating."

"You were good friends?"

"Alas no—although your cousin thinks so." He said good-bye with a lazy, suggestive smile.

Interesting. Rinaldi had managed to suggest both casual acquaintance and erotic entanglement. He even seemed pleased that a supposed frolic with Freddie had broken up Poppy's engagement. Such undiplomatic behavior made me wonder about his agenda, because I certainly didn't believe the current line that Freddie had been a closed book to the other guests.

I broached this on the train. Poppy and I had a compartment to ourselves most of the way, and I asked her about the Tollmans and the Groves.

"I'd seen them around, you know how one does, but I only knew the Larkins—old friends of my parents—and Freddie. Of course, I didn't really know Freddie at all." Her lip trembled and she turned to stare out the window and the fields whipping past. "That was what was so odd," she said after a few minutes.

I waited.

"Do you know that the Tollmans wanted me to ride back to London with them?"

"With Rinaldi?"

"No, even Lea wouldn't go that far. He was their second choice. But Lea was quite insistent with the offer. I explained I had a return ticket and was going back with you. And do you know what she suggested?"

I shook my head.

"That they take my luggage and deliver it. *Save you all the nuisance with porters and such.* I could scarcely keep my bags away from her. What do you think of that?"

I thought that was peculiar, but there are people who love

to take the lead in any crisis. "People don't always know how to show concern."

Poppy sniffed. "Don't be softheaded. Does she strike you as full of concern for anybody but herself?"

I had to admit that Mrs. Tollman had enlivened the weekend with cutting and amusing remarks. She was a woman best taken in small, bracing doses.

"Unless you think she has a hidden heart of gold," Poppy added, and we both laughed.

"They were all odd," I said, though I mentally exempted Jenkins. "Stay away from the country house set. You're far safer in London."

"I met Freddie in London." Poppy turned again to look out the window.

I dropped the subject of the disastrous house party, happy to forget about country living and our unlamented companion and to get my feet back onto pavement.

London is always a tonic for me. I had a jolly reunion with Maurice—he's my Aussie bloke, *bloke* being a proper Aussie word. Maurice is a tall, well-built fellow with a red face that he claims is from his former life in the sun Down Under, but which I know is also from his alcohol consumption, which is impressive. He has dirty-blond hair straggling down to his collar, and when he's in the mood, he wears green corduroy pants with a red sash and an open-necked shirt, so everyone knows he's a bohemian and a queer one at that.

"Here's my Pommy bloke!" he shouted when I walked in

the door. We made use of his model's studio couch before songs (him) and general gaiety (me) and a good deal of wine (both of us). Afterward, I took one of his smaller canvases, dipped into his paints, and started in on Carstairs. I soon commenced swearing: I couldn't get his face at all.

"I really looked, too," I told Maurice, who has been schooling me on the importance of concentration and visual memory. He came and put his hand on my shoulder. I must say that without his shirt and trousers, Maurice really is a proper bloke, and when he suggested a break to "clear your head," that was fine with me. Back for rapture on the studio couch. All very well, I absolutely approve of rapture whenever, but my painting problem remained.

Later, Maurice lit a cigarette and watched the smoke ascend. "Too bad you haven't got a photo."

I was surprised because Maurice believes in disciplining the hand and eye with sketching. Making lines on paper is practically a religious exercise with him.

"Exceptions to every rule," he said. "You could hardly whip out your sketchbook during a police interrogation."

Maurice had been very taken with my role in the police investigation. He's a Catholic who was educated by some robe-wearing order preoccupied with sin, and I wonder if he sees interrogation as related to confession—or maybe the Inquisition. Though he claims he cast off all rules and superstition as soon as his ship left Australia, I'm not so sure. I think he was even a little disappointed that I hadn't spent time in some ghastly nick. I had to recount Inspector Carstairs's examinations more than once, each time producing a telltale gleam in Maurice's eyes. I hoped he wasn't going to become like Armand, my design mentor in Paris, who was an absolutely all-right lover except for his appetite for playacting.

But if Maurice is sometimes focused on what he calls "naughty bits," this time he was being helpful. He began poking around in the studio, lifting drawings, turning over paintings, and shaking painting rags. I really like the studio. If I am honest, the studio is a big part of Maurice's attraction. I like the smell of turpentine and good-quality oils. I like the big professional easel with the crank that raises and lowers canvases and the textured bolts of linen, which I really appreciate now that I've been entrusted with stretching his canvases.

I like the north light from the big, rather dirty windows. I like the paint-encrusted floors and tables, and the jars full of brushes, and the row of palette knives, and the canvases facing the wall. I like their beautiful, whole meal-colored backs and the excitement of turning each one around and seeing the work, even though I'm aware that Maurice is not a top-class painter.

"Here you are!" He had found a newspaper under his easel. It was all spattered with paint, but there on page three was the late Freddie Bosworth, looking as sly as ever, and a shot of Larkin Manor, picturesquely bucolic, and in a boxed insert, my very own Inspector Carstairs, addressing the press. The photo was a small profile, but it helped, and before I had quite corrected the line of the nose and the placement of the eyes, I realized that I would have an even better resource in Nan's scrapbook.

As one of the discoverers of the late Freddie, I'd merited a line in print—sufficient for inclusion in the scrapbook—and if I remembered correctly, there had been a larger shot of Carstairs in the very first report. When I got home, I wasn't disappointed. There was Carstairs's full face in newsprint, and with Nan's magnifying glass, I brought up the pattern of dark and light of his features. I cut out the photo, pinned it to my easel, and started revising the canvas I'd brought from Maurice's studio.

What a difference! Suddenly, I wasn't painting my memory of Carstairs but a rectangle of gray, black, and white that I could distort and exaggerate to bring up the inner man. I worked for several hours with great excitement and enthusiasm, and when I took a break and studied the result, I saw I'd done something interesting.

"Is he capable?" Nan asked with a glance at the easel when she brought in a cup of tea. My nan follows the leading detectives the way punters follow horses.

"I've nothing much to compare him with." The last time police had questioned me about a body had been in a mix of German and English, and I'd been a good deal more upset than I'd been about Freddie.

"I'm surprised you were all allowed to leave so promptly. Not that I wasn't delighted you got home, dear boy."

I gave her a hug. "Goes without saying."

"But it's odd, isn't it?"

"Very, although except for Poppy and me, everyone had an alibi of sorts and lacked an obvious motive. The police were interested in the quarrel between her and Freddie, but I don't think they took it too seriously. The thing is, it must have been hard to kill Freddie, given that he was found practically touching the base of the tower. There was no sign he'd been moved and how anyone except of great size and strength could have surprised him right there and cut his throat is beyond me. And, leaving aside the fact that Poppy is small compared to Freddie and that I am no athlete, making a blood-soaked return unnoticed would have been almost impossible. Larkin Manor has a big and attentive staff."

Nan looked thoughtful. "Lucky about that for you. Could two people have managed it?"

"Don't suggest *that* to the police." My nan sometimes has more imagination than a nanny requires. Of course, that was exactly why she was ideal for me.

"They'd have thought of it themselves if they'd had any sense. Incriminating garments, mysterious bonfires, ashes left in the grate in summertime—" Nan savored the thought, before adding, "Those trip up murderers. Unless there was careful planning."

"I don't think anything could have been planned. Freddie had been due to stay the weekend. After the quarrel with Poppy, he up and asked to be driven to the station for the mid-morning train."

"But he returned. On foot."

"Must have done, unless someone unknown gave him a lift. Thorne, the chauffeur, was back promptly."

"The police need to know why Mr. Bosworth returned. That's the key," said Nan. "Know that, and you'll know who killed him."

A good theory but not a popular one. "Around Larkin Manor, a passing stranger is the favored explanation."

"I'm sure, but most people are murdered by their associates."

Freddie certainly had a wide range of associates. The only problem I could see was that the ones running to grievous bodily harm were mostly back in London. "With the exception of yours truly, all the Larkin Manor guests were people of influence," I suggested.

"Possibly a finger on the scale of justice," agreed my nan. "See you steer clear of that whole outfit."

My intentions exactly.

Over the following days, I worked on my "portrait" of Carstairs, which became more and more what I think of as a real painting, more a thing of pigment and emotion and less a record of a rural inspector, capable or not. Otherwise, I spent nights with Maurice and afternoons in the design showroom: ordinary life, in short. The events at Larkin Manor gradually slipped from my awareness and also from the press. SHOCKING DISCOVERY IN SUSSEX became CONTINUING MYSTERY OF BOSWORTH MURDER before slipping into silence as other sensations claimed the front pages. There was a brief note about a memorial service up north after the body was released, then nothing more.

When I thought that I'd heard the last of Freddie and his unsolved murder, an unexpected visit raised his name again. I was back in my studio, working on a commissioned desk design, when I heard the bell dingle. I'd reached an impasse over the hardware, and I called to Nan that I would take the showroom.

A couple had arrived, a short, plump man in a good suit and a tall woman wearing a beautiful yellow day dress and a black hat with a black dyed pheasant feather. They were looking at the rugs, and I didn't need Nan to tell me this was good solid money.

"Good afternoon," I said.

The woman turned around. "Blimey! It is you!"

I gave her a big hug. "Muriel!"

"The same!" She burst out laughing and kissed me on both cheeks. Muriel saved my life in Berlin in a rather comic fashion. "I saw the name in the paper after the Bosworth murder, but I wasn't sure it was the Francis I knew."

"How well you look. Gorgeous as ever! Still dancing?"

"I'm too old for the Windmill Theater and skimpy costumes. I'm lucky to be retired." She put her hand on the man's shoulder. "Thanks to my husband, Ben, Ben Mendelssohn. My friend Francis. My talented friend! But you got out. With my dress," she added and gave me a poke in the ribs.

A borrowed outfit had aided my escape from a sticky situation.

"The dress came to a bad end, but I'll give you a discount on a rug," I offered.

"A businessman," said her husband in a jovial tone. He had a heavy German accent and an uncertain vocabulary; we conducted the rest of our conversation in a mix of German and English.

That was a profitable afternoon. Herr Mendelssohn had been the proprietor of a furniture store in Berlin. "Mendelssohn's— one of the very best," said Muriel. But he'd read the tea leaves and liquidated his stock. "I made him leave," said Muriel. "I told him I wouldn't marry him anywhere but London." He was now in the East End with a furniture factory, and he turned out to know my suppliers. "Small world," said Muriel.

They bought a rug, and after Ben took a look at my desk design, he made some suggestions and gave me a very fair price for the fabrication. We ended with handshakes all around before tea and scones with Nan. Then Ben stepped out to get a cab and I was left with Muriel for a moment.

"It is so good to see you," I said. "And I like your husband."

Her expression darkened. "He is a good man. I thought he would be safe in London, but now I'm not sure."

"What do you mean?"

"Despite our marriage, Ben is an alien without right of residence here."

"But you are English!"

"Huh," she said. "I am an Englishwoman born and bred, but as Mrs. Mendelssohn, I am a noncitizen."

"That's appalling!"

"Dark Ages stuff. What's worse is Ben had an enemy. That's how we found you. We read in the paper about Freddie Bosworth, and we thought our troubles might be over. But—"

The door opened then and Ben called to Muriel, who gave me a warning look. I went to the street with them and waved goodbye. When they were gone, I was thoughtful. What had Poppy said? *Freddie quite worships Mussolini?* And Mosley. Hadn't she and I nearly quarreled about Oswald and his Blackshirts in the British Union of Fascists, better known as the BUF? Ridiculous acronym and a ridiculous outfit, though maybe not so comic for a refugee Jew in the East End. Not even for a rich one.

Could I see Freddie parading about in a black outfit? Threatening cut-price shopkeepers and harassing political exiles? Not likely somehow. Behind the scenes where there was money lying about? That was another matter, and I thought about the country house party that had featured an Italian diplomat, an ex-government functionary from the City, a furniture manufacturer, several fascist sympathizers, and Freddie.

Poppy and yours truly were the only people—unless one exempted the major, whose whole interest appeared to be architectural—without connections to Conservative politics, the Italians, the BUF, or big money. I decided to see Poppy as soon as possible. She'd gone back to her family's home just off Sloane Square, so I sent a note there.

The response came in the morning and Poppy herself appeared in the showroom a few hours later. She was wearing a plaid dress in muted colors, a jaunty red hat, and matching heels. She came into the studio and gave me a kiss before wandering around, lifting my sketches, examining the pencils, and pulling strands out of the hanks of wool samples.

"Mother's been driving me crazy."

I shrugged. I'm unfamiliar with maternal anxiety.

"Oh, and she wanted to be remembered to you."

"Greetings to Mater." Perhaps I'd come up in Aunt Theresa's estimation. "So are you going to move back to your flat?"

At this, she crossed her arms with a nervous gesture. "I'm frightened, Francis. I don't know what to do. I can't stand living at home much longer, but I'm nervous every time I'm at the flat."

"That's maybe natural, Poppy. You've had a terrible shock. Two, really."

"That's not it," she said sharply. "I'm over Freddie, believe me. No, I'm being watched. I know I am. When I'm on the street, sometimes, I'll see a car or a man. And then I'll see the same car, the same man again a few blocks later. If I take notice, the car pulls out and drives off."

"And the man?"

"I've seen him in Harrods twice, and each time, I've had the feeling he'd followed me inside. I've noticed him outside our house, too, hanging about, smoking, and I saw him again yesterday, walking in the park. I am sure it's the same man. I never really see his face because he wears a fedora pulled down, but I recognize him. Something about his walk, as if he might have a bad back, something stiff and distinctive. Same man, same out-of-date brown suit, same brown hat with a stained band."

I thought there must be fifty thousand men in London sporting roughly the same wardrobe.

"You think I'm a nervous Nellie," she said, "but here's the other thing: Someone has been in my flat."

"Besides your landlady, you mean?"

"My landlady does not leave a smell of . . . motor oil, I think it is. It smells like Major Larkin's garage when Thorne's been working on the car. And that's not all. I've a blouse missing."

"Poppy, you have a bedroom in your parents' house and one at your flat and closets and bureaus in both. Likely the blouse's just gone missing in the laundry."

"No. I went first to my flat, remember, when we came back from Sussex? I left the clothes I'd worn at the Larkins there. I never wanted to wear them again, especially that wretched blouse and skirt I'd had on when we found Freddie. Just the look of them makes me feel sick."

"You didn't chuck them to the rag and bone man, did you?"

"I wish I had. Two weeks ago, I went to the flat to pick up these shoes. When I unlocked the door, there was an odd smell, and I could tell that someone had gone through my things. The blouse was missing. Not the skirt, just the blouse. Like you, I assumed I'd been mistaken. I checked at home and asked about the laundry. Annie hadn't seen the blouse, although she remembered it, because she'd monogrammed in for me when I first got it. The whole thing bothered me enough that I stopped on the way here and checked again. No blouse and—I don't know, Francis—just a sense that someone had disarranged things. Carefully maybe, but disarranged just the same."

"What did your landlady say?"

"She was very put out, insisted that she'd let no one into the flat."

I thought that's what she would say and also that various clever folk could open a door without a key.

"She said the smell was probably gas, and she'd have the company check the line."

"It's possible, Poppy."

"Possible, yes. But I want you to come to the flat with me," she said. "I want to see what you think."

CHAPTER 4

Poppy's flat was in a converted town house not far from the British Museum, a four-story white stone building with a handsome front entrance and an overgrown back garden. Poppy was on the second floor, two rooms, plus kitchenette, bathroom, and WC, rather posh. Despite her complaints about her mother, Poppy enjoyed a sizable allowance; I could see why Freddie had been tempted.

We went through the flat carefully. Any smell of oil or gas had dissipated, her landlady having aired the place, and everything looked spotlessly neat. I couldn't see anything amiss.

"It's just a feeling," Poppy kept saying. "See here." She opened a drawer with various lacy underthings, her little leather contraceptive box, and a pretty lavender sachet. "My governess trained me to be neat."

The slips and panties and such were not jumbled together but not folded perfectly, either. I lifted the top layer of garments one by one, set them aside, and started on the second layer before I noticed a faint oily black smear on one of the slips. "Have you been doing engine repair in your skivvies?" I sniffed the fabric; under the pervasive odor of lavender and French cologne was a hint of petrol. "Too bad it's not a fingerprint."

"I was right! I knew it."

"So your apartment's been searched. What's missing?"

"Nothing. Nothing at all. That's what frightens me, Francis. Burglary, I understand. I don't understand this at all. Is it to scare me? Someone who blames me for Freddie's death?"

"I doubt Freddie had such devoted friends." I sat down on one end of her bed. "Freddie returned that day after he'd given every indication that he was leaving for good. Right?"

She nodded.

"So why come back? Was he hoping to be reconciled with you?"

She shook her head. "I don't think so."

I didn't, either. Freddy had certainly seemed angry but not at all like a man with a broken heart. "I agree, because, otherwise, wouldn't he have called from the station and had Thorne collect him? What about his luggage?"

"Left at the station," said Poppy. "The inspector had me identify the bags."

"So he wasn't returning to stay. He hadn't changed his mind about that."

"He came back to see someone else?" Poppy suggested.

"Or for something he'd left. Could he have forgotten something important in the heat of the moment?"

"Same objection," said Poppy. "Why not call and get picked up? Or better yet, ask Thorne to deliver whatever it was to the station?"

Good question. I took a breath. "You remember that when I warned you about Freddie, I wasn't terribly specific."

"You were damn unspecific." Poppy found her cigarettes and lighted up.

"I only indicated that he had a bad reputation."

"You certainly didn't tell me that he was buggering Italian diplomats."

"Diplomatic sex, per se, is not immoral in my book, but there were some nasty rumors. No matter what he hinted about family properties up north or in Ireland or wherever, Freddie had to earn a living. How he did that was mysterious, and one suggestion was blackmail."

Poppy looked at me. "He was threatening a kiss-and-tell book like a fading actress?"

"More likely he was set to contact the tabloids. Perhaps with photos to sell."

Poppy sat down beside me, her shoulders slumped, and said nothing for a moment. "You think he was blackmailing someone at the Larkins' party?"

"It's a possibility."

"One of his friends?"

"Friends of a sort. They've certainly made it clear since that they hardly knew him. Perhaps he'd hidden the evidence and forgotten to collect it."

"That creepy Rinaldi killed him!" she exclaimed, leaping up again. "He used a knife like the Borgias! It fits, Francis! It does!"

"The Borgias preferred poison, but I think Rinaldi took

another approach." I told her about spotting the Italian at the door of Freddie's room. "He pretended to be returning a book."

"Ha, that's rich! That is a lie! Freddie never read anything but the papers and only politics and the racing results. He was even more ignorant than I am, and that's saying something." She went on a bit about her faithless fiancé, whom she'd surprised in the garden with Rinaldi, a suggestive but not conclusive scene. She hadn't been convinced until she saw Freddie at the door of Rinaldi's room on the morning they went riding. He'd claimed to be settling up a few pounds after a card game.

"Owed to him or to Rinaldi?" I asked.

"What does it matter!" she cried. "Everything was a lie with Freddie! A man should at least be faithful before marriage."

A Wildean note for certain! I interrupted her discourse on fidelity and marriage. "Do think for a minute, Poppy. I have a reason for asking."

"To Rinaldi," she said. "Why?"

"Peter Tollman thinks Freddie was killed for the money he was carrying, because he had won big at cards the night before."

"I knew that Freddie was lying!"

"Or else Tollman lied about Freddie's winning. Didn't the papers say that his wallet was virtually empty?"

"I think. But why lie about a card game anyway?" she exclaimed. "And why did someone search my apartment and who's following me in the street?" She turned around in agitation and looked out the window.

"Was Freddie in your room at the Larkins?"

"Grow up! Of course he was." And she made a face.

"If he had something to hide . . ."

"Oh!" Her expression changed. Despite her anger, she really still hadn't thought that badly of Freddie. "In my things, you mean. How absolutely rotten of him!"

"It's a possibility. Or maybe he didn't, but whoever killed him has come up empty and thinks that he might have."

"He's jolly well out of luck in that case!"

"Not necessarily," I said. "You've been staying at your mother's house. You've probably taken clothes, things, back and forth. We'd better have a look through your room at home."

"Today's Mother's bridge afternoon. No one will be home."

That sounded ideal to me. Aunt Theresa has never been a favorite of mine, and I'm sure she'd say the same of me. We walked over to the square and up the front steps to the Dinesmor house, big, solid, and comfortable. Poppy let us in with her key. "Maids' day off," she said.

Poppy's bedroom was on the second floor to the back, a fine square room with big windows, a fireplace, and a window seat. Her canopy bed was frilly with white linen and flanked by pictures showing favorite horses festooned with the many ribbons she'd won from pony up to novice hunter competitions. She had a stool covered in cowhide and supported by legs and hooves. She had a nice bamboo rocking chair and a pretty Aubusson rug and fine striped wallpaper. A hockey stick leaned next to the door, and the single bookshelf held a collection of scrapbooks and schoolgirl albums.

"Don't you dare open those," Poppy said. "Too juvenile for words."

Closet first. A very enviable evening cape in midnight velvet. "Practically an antique," Poppy said. Assorted dresses, none
with pockets. We paid particular attention to the clothes she had
brought back from Larkin Manor but came up empty-handed.
Ditto the drawers, her jewelry case, her toiletries bag. We opened
the top of the window seat. We looked under the bed. Nothing
dropped, nothing lost. Maybe we were wrong. Maybe Freddie
had returned to the house for other reasons entirely.

Finally, Poppy picked up her purse and said, "Let's go out for
tea and cakes. My treat."

As we walked toward Sloane Square, a breeze swept along the
pavement and ruffled through the trees. Several cabs passed us,
along with delivery boys pedaling heavy bikes with big wicker
baskets of vegetables, fruit, bread, or meat. A neighbor waved
to Poppy just as a motorbike, grumbling behind us, accelerated.
The driver hopped the machine onto the sidewalk and, before
either of us could react, grabbed the purse hanging from Poppy's
shoulder and accelerated again.

The force of the machine hurled Poppy to the cement and
started to drag her.

"Let it go! Let go!" I shouted, before the strap was wrenched
from her hand and the machine leaped off the curb and roared away.

Both my cousin's legs were bleeding; her jacket was torn, and
she had a scuff down the left side of her face. She sat on the sidewalk for a minute, clearly stunned. I was helping her up when a
woman bustled from one of the houses.

"I saw that!" she called. "I'll ring the police. Bring your friend
inside."

"I'm perfectly all right," Poppy said, and she repeated that twice. But it took both me and the stout, corseted lady of the house to help her up the steps and into the front hallway.

"Sit yourself down," the woman said. "I'll get the police."

We heard her calling. She was Mrs. Lionel Partinger and she was shocked and angry. The "young woman" was injured, bleeding. The "demon motorcyclist" had been speeding, and, worst of all, I suspected, "this outrageous attack" had occurred right at her front door. "Of course, I saw everything. I was just stepping outside!" she concluded. Footsteps in the hall and a pause before she returned with a shot of brandy and a basin of water.

"Drink up and take your stockings off before the blood dries," she said to Poppy. "And you"—meaning me—"wait on the stoop for the police." She issued commands like a ward matron, and we did what we were told.

Within minutes, a beanpole tall and spider gangly constable arrived to park his high black bicycle against the railings. He took my name, address, and a short account before we went inside where we found Poppy looking a little better. Her color had returned and the dizzy shock had passed, for she was sitting up straight with a cup of tea. Her torn and bloody stockings lay dead on the floor, and even with the blood wiped from her bare legs, her oozing knees and long abrasions showed how far she had been dragged along the walk.

"A nasty business, miss," said the constable.

She nodded, cradling her left arm. The elbow was gone from the jacket on that side, and at the very least, I guessed poor Poppy had severe bruising. And she is left-handed, too.

"She needs to see a doctor," said Mrs. Partinger. "And something other than a bicycle to get her there."

"I'm fine to walk," Poppy protested.

"You'll have your legs bleeding," said Mrs. Partinger, and I agreed this was not a good plan.

"I'll take a cab," Poppy said, before she remembered the loss of her purse.

"Much money in it, miss?" the constable asked.

"A few shillings. Not even a pound."

"Odd business," he said, closing up his notebook. He asked to use the phone and was directed to the alcove at the end of the hall.

"Now," said Mrs. Partinger, "is there someone to be notified?"

Poppy nodded reluctantly. "Mother, I guess. She'll make a frightful fuss."

"A mother's privilege," said Mrs. Partinger in a tone that brooked no denial.

"She can pick me up in a cab," Poppy said. "If it's not a trouble for me to wait here?"

"Nonsense. We'll use my small sitting room. But bandages, first, now everything's been cleaned." She left us for a moment, returning with iodine, gauze, and tape. "The iodine will sting," she warned and began dabbing Poppy's legs, bringing tears to her eyes. "This takes me back," Mrs. Partinger said.

"You've done nursing?" I asked, mostly to distract Poppy.

"Forward dressing stations in the Ardennes." For a moment, her face darkened. "Nothing so serious here anyway," she told Poppy. "But the arm should be looked to. You could have a hairline fracture. Your doctor will want to check your eyes, too. Just to make sure your head is all right."

"I've taken worse falls from horses," Poppy said, recovering a little of her spirit.

Mrs. Partinger stood up. "I'm sure you have, but this is different. You were hurt deliberately. You keep after the police to find out why."

My aunt Theresa arrived with a good deal of comment and excitement to whisk Poppy off to their local GP, where Mrs. Partinger was proved accurate: My cousin had a hairline fracture and a possible concussion. She was to stay quiet for a few days, or, as she put it, under "house arrest and strict surveillance," a sentence that included bridge with her mother's friends every afternoon.

When I arrived a few days later, bearing some of Nan's scones—*I know what their cook's are like*, said Nan—Poppy's face lit up.

"Oh, Francis! You're a prince and a savior!" She sat up straighter on her frilly bed. Even under a good deal of makeup, the livid bruise down the side of her face and the dark swelling around her left eye were all too visible. Her chewed-up legs were hidden in a smart pair of slacks and her left arm was in a sling. "I'd break right out of here if I didn't feel like I've been run over by a cement mixer."

I sympathized and told her amusing stories (amusing in retrospect, that is) of a time in Berlin when I'd collected broken ribs under similar circumstances. Poppy looked thoughtful when I was finished. "Perhaps it wasn't robbery at all," she said. "We didn't look terribly rich, did we?"

"Certainly, I didn't."

"Did you get a look at him?"

I shook my head. "No chance. He was wearing goggles and a cap pulled down."

Just then, the doorbell rang. We heard Annie in the hall and low masculine voices.

"Would you see who that is, Francis?"

I leaned over the hall railing to meet Inspector Carstairs's gaze. Next to him was another man, also in plainclothes, showing Annie his identity card. "You'd better come up," I said, and the two mounted the stairs.

"Inspector Carstairs," Poppy said, "I didn't expect to see you. The local constable is investigating. Supposedly."

"This is Inspector Davis from the Met, but we aren't here directly about your injuries."

"I should think you would be!" Aunt Theresa had appeared in the doorway, and she had a lot to say about Poppy's injuries and the activities of the Met. When Inspector Carstairs explained that new evidence had been uncovered and that Poppy would be needed to identify it, my aunt warmed up on his entirely unwarranted intrusion, with an aside about my presence. By the time she was finished, Poppy would have been ready to accompany white slavers, never mind respectable coppers.

"Nonsense, Mother. I'm stiff and sore, but if I can help in any way with the investigation, I'm ready to go."

"You should have a lawyer," I said, for new evidence, two detectives, and a trip to Sussex all raised alarms for me.

Wrong remark. My aunt went from indignation to high

dudgeon. A respectable young lady had nothing to worry about from any police inquiry ever. "But you can make yourself useful, Francis," she concluded. "This is partly your fault, as you were with Penelope at that disastrous house party. Go down to Sussex with her. A member of the family should be there, and I trust this time that you'll keep her from disaster."

I sensed a fallacy in this plan, but Inspector Carstairs pronounced the arrangement "ideal" with something approaching enthusiasm.

I helped Poppy into her coat, her mother fetched a purse, and we departed in an unmarked car for an awkward ride down to Sussex. Poppy and I sat in the back, the two inspectors up front. Carstairs concentrated on the driving, but the man from the Met made himself agreeable, all the better to ask questions informally.

Inspector Davis was younger than our rural inspector and dressed much more smartly. He had strong, even features in a square face, rather large and protuberant eyes, and a round, bold skull that kept him a few degrees from elegance. He wanted to know if Poppy ever carried substantial sums of money or wore valuable jewelry that might have attracted the man on the motorcycle. Poppy shook her head.

"Maybe he wasn't after money," she said and proceeded to explain that her flat had been searched, mentioning the missing blouse. At this, Carstairs took a quick look in his rearview mirror, but neither he nor Inspector Davis followed up the information until we reached his local station, a two-story smoke-blackened brick building that opened to a dark reception area and holding cells down one corridor and interview rooms down another. The whole place was permeated by a smell of stale sweat and smoke, and when Poppy took my arm, I felt her heart. My cousin lacks imagination. I think until that moment, she hadn't anticipated anything worse than inconvenience. The station underlined not just Freddie's death but her own danger. "What a dreadful place!"

"Be prepared," I said, but with the two inspectors and a constable bearing mugs of tea, I had no chance to give her better warning before we were ushered to an interview room. The four of us sat down at the scarred green table. A young uniformed officer sat a little behind us with a notepad. This had a very official feel. I was tempted to interrupt and insist on a solicitor for Poppy, but my cousin was wearing a determined look, suggesting that even good advice might be ignored.

Inspector Carstairs put his large hands on the table. "There have been developments," he said. "Following the autopsy report."

I hadn't expected that.

"The guests at Larkin Manor were more or less ruled out either by alibis or by the difficulty of fatally slashing a man of his size and strength so close to the wall of the tower. However, Mr. Bosworth must have fallen—or was pushed—from the top of the ruin. The autopsy revealed a severe head injury as well as damage to his spine. He was probably unconscious when his throat was cut."

"That's horrible," said Poppy. "That's almost worse to think about."

Horrible, indeed, for I realized that alibis or not, any one of the guests could have managed to dispatch him.

"As you see," the inspector continued, "this very much

changes our views on who might physically have been able to commit the murder."

Poppy nodded.

"Then we have this," Carstairs said, and he opened a paper parcel sitting on the scarred green table.

Inside was a plain mauve silk blouse with short sleeves and pearl buttons and a big, almost black, swath of what I guessed was dried blood.

"Do you recognize it?" Inspector Carstairs asked Poppy.

She had gone quite pale, but if my cousin lacks imagination, she makes up for it with courage. "It looks like my missing blouse," she said, voice steady. "Annie puts my initials on all my things—back of the collar."

The inspector turned the blouse, revealing script initials embroidered in slightly darker silk. Annie is a fine seamstress.

"It's mine. I had it at the Larkins, but I never wore it, and as I told Inspector Davis in the car, that blouse has been missing for well over a week, closer to two."

"We have a problem then," said Carstairs. "Given the blood."

"It is human?" I asked.

"Very definitely."

"But you can't tell whose, can you?"

"Who else's would it be than Freddie Bosworth's?"

"But I didn't have it on at the Larkins!" exclaimed Poppy. "Not even for a minute. It turned out not to match my tweed skirt."

"Odd it should turn up now," I said. "When your men searched the property so carefully."

"Indeed," said Carstairs.

"Could we ask where it was found?"

Carstairs thought for a moment before he said, "Major Larkin was having some repairs done on the little banqueting house floor. A carpenter found the blouse under a loose board and reported it, given its proximity to the murder scene."

The idea was ridiculous. Poppy had supposedly pushed Freddie off the tower, slashed his throat (with what convenient knife?), and stashed the bloodstained blouse in the banqueting house. I expected her to burst out laughing, but she looked shocked.

"You can't seriously think that Poppy walked back, bloody and half naked, across the north lawn without anyone seeing her?" I asked.

"Perhaps she changed in the banqueting house," the inspector suggested. "Perhaps she had hidden another garment there."

"That little house was kept locked. When the major gave me the tour, he opened it with an impressive key."

Carstairs gave a half smile and produced another paper parcel. "Like this?" he asked, revealing a key that certainly looked like the major's prize artifact.

"You've tried it in the lock?"

"Of course. It was in the victim's pocket."

Why hadn't I searched Freddie's pockets when I had the chance! I glanced at Poppy, who didn't meet my eye.

"Well?" asked the inspector.

"I did not kill Freddie," Poppy said. "I was never up in the tower, and I certainly didn't hide that blouse. But Francis is right. I should have a solicitor."

She pushed back her chair and stood up. I did, too, half expecting the command to sit down.

"That is your right," Inspector Davis said smoothly. "But"— and here he looked at his watch—"it's late in the day. Too late to contact your local solicitor and have someone come down from London. You'll have to remain here."

"Not in one of your ghastly cells!"

"We'll find somewhere in town," I said, though I was uncertain that would be allowed even if we managed to pay for it.

Poppy had another idea. "I'll call the Larkins. They're old friends of my family even if they did find the blouse. Eveline will put us up. That will be all right, won't it, Inspector?"

I expected a quick denial, but Davis said that was a capital idea and Carstairs offered to phone the Larkins for us. "You can call your mother yourself," he added, "and arrange for legal advice."

CHAPTER 5

Rain completed my joy when we arrived at Larkin Manor. Inspector Davis had taken charge of us, and when he dropped us off, I saw that he and the major were obviously acquainted. The old camaraderie of the trenches? Or some other connection? For Poppy's sake, I wanted to know, and I tried to rouse myself to find out.

But it is difficult to do anything when I so dislike the country. Especially in rain, which creates mud and brings up all the odors of horse and cow and dog that make my head hurt. Give me the artificial life of London any day of the week.

Poppy, now, is a different sort. Here, where her engagement blew up, where her faithless ex-fiancé was slaughtered, and where she, herself, lay under suspicion of a capital crime, she took a deep breath and smiled. "Country air," she said.

The Larkins were included in her joy. She gave Eveline an exuberant hug, and the major, too, and immediately asked about Yankee, the gelding she'd ridden on her visit. "Thriving," said the major, "and there's a new filly I want you to see."

With that, they set off to the stables, Poppy in a borrowed pair of Wellies, the better to tromp through stalls and wade into pastures. I was left with Eveline Larkin, who I expected would direct me to my room with as few of her precious words as possible. But I was wrong. Assuring me that Jenkins would find me an evening jacket (as if this had been my worry) and some toiletries, Mrs. Larkin led me into the library. A fire was burning in the grate, and I was invited to sit on one of the big leather sofas.

"How good of you to come down with Penelope," she said, her voice almost without expression. Even her compliments had a cool edge.

"She would have been better off with a lawyer, but you can't tell Poppy much. And Aunt Theresa even less."

"There's no question about Penelope's innocence." Eveline phrased it as a statement, but I heard it as a question. And *Penelope*. She had been *Poppy* to the Larkins just three weeks before. *Be careful, Francis!*

"Of course not," I said, trying for indignation, although, in fact, I was surprised that Poppy had been allowed out of the station. Another thing that merited consideration.

"I'm sure she doesn't need a lawyer," Eveline repeated. "When she has family and friends. You can be sure the major and I will do everything in our power."

"Poppy will appreciate that." She would certainly have more belief in their goodwill than I had. "The blouse that turned up. You know, I could swear Poppy never wore it here."

"Young ladies change their clothes so often, don't they? All the better to dazzle their young men." Her frightful smile made me wonder if she had ever been flirtatious. If so, she was seriously out of practice. Realizing that or else sensing that she'd picked the wrong target, she abruptly switched gears. "I can tell you finding her blouse was a terrific shock for Magnus."

"The major found it himself?" That was not what the police had told us.

"Who else? He was inspecting the building, prying up some boards to get ready for Bailey. Ever since the war, our local carpenter has charged the most frightful prices, perfectly criminal, so Magnus takes on some of the work himself. Anyway, Magnus was checking a rotten board, and there it was. Blood-soaked," she concluded.

Although I thought that an old friend convinced of Poppy's innocence might have lost that piece of evidence, I agreed it was shocking. "But puzzling," I added, "if we are agreed Poppy is not to blame."

"I am sure there is an explanation," Eveline said.

"The simplest explanation is that someone wishes to frame my cousin."

"Unthinkable!"

"There aren't too many alternatives," I said. "A 'passing stranger' would have been hard-pressed to steal one of Poppy's blouses."

Eveline Larkin expressed her displeasure with this analysis, and she left the library in such a huff that I had to find the housekeeper to locate my room. Predictably, dinner was an awkward affair. Miss Victoria Larkin was away appreciating culture and fascism in Rome. The gossipy old cousin had returned home. We were strictly en famille at dinner.

Poppy, looking quite smart in a borrowed frock, talked horses with the major as if she hadn't a care in the world, while Eveline and I sought for neutral topics without much success. Given the circumstances, it's surprising that only one moment really made me uneasy.

Major Larkin had just finished a long anecdote about a point-to-point race on a headstrong mare, when Eveline turned to Poppy. "How is Theresa?"

"Mother's fine," Poppy said. "I told her we were staying over. She thanks you profusely and apologizes for my informal clothes."

"It is our pleasure." The major reached over to pat her hand. "We'll get this sorted out jolly soon."

"A quiet resolution," Eveline agreed, "is much desired by all parties."

"Has your mother arranged for a solicitor? You were quite right when you told the police you wanted one," I said.

Poppy frowned. "Time enough for that tomorrow."

"No need to trouble your mother about that. My solicitor here can look into the matter," the major said quickly. "Clarkson's a good man. He's helping me in negotiations with the National Trust. Larkin Manor's so integral to the fabric of the county that we must make plans for its preservation. Even though there is no entail." He turned to Poppy, "You see, my dear, the Larkins did not have the old prejudices against female inheritance."

"I am glad to hear that," said Poppy, "and Victoria must be, too."

"I think a flat in Bloomsbury or Chelsea might suit Victoria better." Eveline's voice was dry, as if her husband's enthusiasms found little echo from her.

"Victoria will do her duty by the estate," the major said. "And Clarkson will see that the Trust handles the manor. You can't think how complicated it is to preserve the treasures of England." Once launched on his favorite topic, the major was unstoppable. The possibility of the hangman's noose for Poppy was a minor detail when weighed against the upkeep of the manor, which the major hoped to arrange at public expense with minimal interference.

This interesting topic took us right through dessert, coffee, and liqueurs, and as we were so few, we all sat together in the salon for what seemed to me an interminable time, made worse by the fact that the butler, rather than my agreeable friend Jenkins, was serving. Finally, Poppy pleaded fatigue, and I took the opportunity to go upstairs with her.

"You haven't yet gotten a solicitor?" I asked as soon as we were out of earshot.

Her eyes slid away. "I didn't want to worry Mother."

"Aunt Theresa will be a lot more worried if you wind up in a cell. You turned quite white when Carstairs mentioned the banqueting house."

"I'd met Freddie there. Once on a previous visit. And the day of the argument, he'd been after me to meet him someplace quiet, to talk things out, you know. Maybe he already had the key; I'll bet he did. When the inspector mentioned it, I couldn't help thinking—I don't know what. A bad moment is all, and anyway, the major said—"

"Poppy! This Clarkson chap is the major's solicitor. He's going to act in the Larkins' best interests, which may not be the same as yours. There's something else you should know, too. It wasn't the carpenter who found that wretched blouse. Eveline said that it was the major himself."

She was surprised at that, and she stopped at the door of her room. I stepped inside and pulled the door closed behind us.

"Does it matter?" Poppy asked, although her face suggested it did. "He would have to tell the police, wouldn't he?"

"Maybe, but maybe not, if he's as convinced of your innocence as he claims."

"He does believe me. I know he does."

I reserved judgment on that. "Something else I noticed. He and Inspector Davis know each other. Quite well, I'm guessing."

"Hunting, horses, historic preservation—the major belongs to all sorts of organizations. Or maybe he and the inspector served together. He keeps up with his old regiment."

"Still, why is the Met involved at all? Carstairs seems thorough and capable."

"I don't know, Francis! I don't know why you think *I* would know." Poppy whipped out her cigarettes and lit one greedily. She was not as calm as she'd seemed at dinner.

"I'm worried. You need legal advice, because innocence isn't always enough. You and your mother and Eveline are ignoring the damage this can do even if you are eventually cleared."

"What does Eveline have to do with it?"

"Earlier, she was on about how you didn't need a solicitor."

"I see." Poppy looked thoughtful but added nothing more.

"The major, when you were with the horses, did he say anything about the case or about Freddie?"

Poppy shook her head. "I'm tired, Francis. It will be time enough in the morning for all this."

With that, Poppy turned mulish and I gave up. I changed out of my borrowed dinner clothes and, using their return as an excuse, ventured down the back stairs in search of the agreeable footman, the only person who could redeem the dismal evening. Instead, I met the butler, who gave me to understand that I might have left the clothes in my room. As for my desire to thank Jenkins, no thanks were required, and he was otherwise engaged.

Let your imagination go, Francis! Disappointed, I went to bed alone, intermittently disturbed by the wind and rain that beat against the house until a pale and watery morning dawned.

Below my windows, weak sunlight reflected in the puddles: Poppy would want to ride. Possibly, she was already out.

Downstairs, I had tea, an egg, and toast. The major came in, followed by the butler with the morning papers.

"You're not riding, Major?"

"Not this morning. Penelope said she would have to be ready to return to the police station early." He opened the *Times* and disappeared behind its folds. I went to the library and checked the morning from the garden terrace. Dry now, though the fields would be wet and the lanes, muddy. When I returned to the breakfast room, Poppy still hadn't appeared. The major offered me *The Daily Express*, and I sat down to read the news of the day à la Beaverbrook.

Eight o'clock. Poppy must have overslept, not too surprising under the circumstances. I went upstairs, noticed that the bathroom was empty, and tapped softly on her door. "Poppy?"

No answer. Inside, the curtains were drawn; the room, chilly and still. Alarmed, I opened a drape. The bed was rumpled but empty. Perhaps Poppy was on an early morning visit to the horses, her most reliable consolation.

Or else she'd made a run for it, suggesting— I shook my head. I refused to think she was guilty. Frightened, maybe, for the whole business had unsettled her, though more likely defiant. I'd seen her often enough on the hunting field to know that she was willful and brave. But if she was innocent, running was as foolish as failing to hire a solicitor. What had looked like confident innocence was now going to put her in a bad light.

Another thought: What if she had been lured, or forced, from the house? Better in some ways, much worse in others, suggesting that she, like Freddie, had gone to a dangerous meeting or that someone wanted her temporarily—or permanently—out of the way. Wasn't that more likely than that, bruised and scraped as she was, Poppy had set out through mud and wet to catch the early train? I ran down the service stairs to see if the Wellies she'd borrowed the day before were still in the back entry.

Riding boots, gardening shoes, a variety of Wellies, including a pair that looked to be Poppy's size. Had she walked the few miles to the station in her dress shoes? Or had a friend with a car run down to Sussex in the wee hours of the morning? Though I doubted that Aunt Theresa would be part of such a scheme, I couldn't rule out her deb friends, madcap lassies who careened around London on scavenger hunts with equally silly boyfriends.

If she'd gone with one of them, she was safe for the moment. I was trying to decide how likely that was when I heard a familiar voice in the front hall. Back up the service stairs to descend to the main hall like a proper guest. Inspector Carstairs was in the breakfast room with the major. The inspector was holding an unlit cigarette, and so far as he ever looked eager for anything, he looked eager for his next hit of nicotine. "Good morning, Mr. Bacon."

"Morning, Inspector."

"Is Penelope ready?" the major asked me.

I took a breath. I still hadn't decided whether it was better to stall or to raise the alarm. It would have helped if my cousin had confided her plans to me. "Poppy isn't in her room. She must have gone for a walk."

"Nonsense! We'd have heard her on the stairs. She's about the house somewhere. Taking counsel with Eveline, I expect." The major pushed back his chair and went up to disturb his wife, who seldom saw the light of day before ten or eleven.

He returned looking puzzled and concerned. "The staff didn't hear her go out, either," he reported. "That means she's probably been gone for several hours."

"The station's within walking distance. If she caught the early train up to London, we can catch her at Victoria." Carstairs went off to phone the train station, apparently without success, for when he got off the phone, he announced that the house and grounds would have to be searched. He and his sergeant proceeded to go through the house, top to bottom, before investigating the garage, stables, and barns. All the cars were in the garage, but Carstairs still made a point of asking me if Poppy could drive. I said I had no idea as neither her mother nor Freddie had owned a car.

There were no prints of her heels in the lane, and no sign of my cousin in the stable and no missing hunter, either. Even the old pony was safe in its stall.

Back in the house, Eveline had arisen, very cranky, to confirm that she hadn't seen Penelope since the previous evening. The butler, cook, housekeeper, and chambermaids confirmed the major's account: They had not seen Miss Penelope leave the house. My friend Jenkins was doing early errands in the village. I wondered if there was any connection, and maybe Carstairs did, too, because he said that he'd wait.

The major went off to work in his office, first escorting Carstairs and me to the smoking room, a venue that completed my happiness. Dogs, horses, cows, pollen, farm dust, and smoke: the asthmatic's dream combination! Plus a guardian of the law. This was certainly my lucky day.

The inspector puffed up a storm, and when he had established the requisite cloud of smoke, he turned to me. "Where is your cousin?"

"I wish I knew."

"I believe she trusts you," he said carefully.

"I know she does, and that's why I'm worried. She didn't even hint about leaving."

"Ah." Carstairs studied the end of his cigarette for a moment. "The simplest explanation is that your cousin, being guilty, has decided to make a run for it."

"I don't believe that, and I don't believe she panicked, either."

"Your reasoning, aside from family loyalty?"

"The fact that you can't believe she's guilty. If you did, you would have charged her yesterday or found some excuse to hold her."

Carstairs studied me for a moment. "We will talk more at the station," he said.

I wanted to return to work and, failing that, to help search for Poppy. He dismissed both possibilities with a wave and disappeared into the service quarters. I guessed that Jenkins had returned with a satisfactory explanation, for Carstairs soon reappeared to announce that we were to meet his colleague from the Met. His sergeant had the police car waiting to take us to the station.

Back to the interview room. We were three this time, Carstairs, Davis, and yours truly. "We have some problems," said Davis.

"You'll have more when my aunt learns Poppy's missing."

He ignored this. "You may be our best hope of finding her quickly."

I was uneasy. I find it hard to be cooperative with officials who see me as a civic undesirable and a potential boost to their arrest rate. "I don't know where she is, but I'm sure she didn't kill Freddie."

"We will reserve judgment on that. We have considerable circumstantial evidence."

"Equally strong for the whole house party, I would think. But how many people arrive for a weekend equipped with a lethal knife?"

"Exactly. And the attack on your cousin, severe enough to appear genuine, plus her claim that someone searched her flat, might lead us in a different direction."

"You might have assured Poppy of that yesterday!"

"Her disappearance, however, casts a different light on every-thing. Suggesting strongly that she may have something to hide."

"Or that someone was anxious to get her out of the way. She should never have been without police protection."

"There were complications," Davis said irritably.

He didn't elaborate, and Carstairs continued. "What interests us at the moment is that someone made an effort to implicate your cousin with that bloodstained blouse, as well as with highly colored accounts of her relationship with Mr. Bosworth."

How could they be surprised? "Aside from me, everyone who heard them arguing was Freddie's friend. Naturally, they put him in the best possible light."

"You did not consider him a friend?" Davis asked.

"I considered him dishonest and unreliable. I thought Poppy was making a colossal mistake."

"Then you knew him?" the inspector asked slyly.

"Knew enough about him."

"Lover's jealousy, perhaps?"

Careful, Francis. When I said nothing, Davis added, "Your habits, Mr. Bacon, are known."

"Then you'll know that my contact with Freddie was a casual one. He was handsome, but blackmail was one of the nicer rumors going around. I had no time for him—or for his politics."

When Davis smiled, I realized that in my anxiety for Poppy, I had maybe said too much.

"We have another possibility: a devoted cousin who knows a former lover's reputation and decides to prevent that 'colossal mistake.'"

"I suppose that 'devoted cousin' also stole Poppy's blouse, soaked it in Freddie's blood, jimmied the banqueting house lock, and planted the bloodstained evidence to implicate her. I don't think that will hold up at all."

"No," said Davis. "Not in the long run. But you own a design studio that's profitable enough to support you and an old retainer. Such concerns depend on the luxury trade, don't they?"

"Good design isn't cheap," I said, but my heart sank.

"Your business lives on reputation, and while notoriety can be an asset in certain situations, you're in a precarious spot."

I'm always in a precarious spot; I'm beginning to think it's my natural environment. "What do you want?"

"Why, your help as a citizen," Davis said promptly. "We need to find who killed Bosworth, and to do that, we need to know more about his contacts. Outside the country house set."

"Fine, but you must find Poppy. I'm afraid that either she did not leave willingly or she was apprehended on the way to the station. And, really, she shouldn't have been at the Larkins at all. You didn't have enough to charge her, and both of us had identified the blouse, so why weren't we returned to London?"

Inspector Davis, like Carstairs, resorted to a cigarette. He lit up, blew out the match, and said, "There are other dimensions to the case."

I didn't like the sound of that. "Dimensions of concern to the Met? Or some other agency?"

"You might say that."

"You put my cousin in danger," I said, beginning to get angry. "For reasons that have nothing to do with any evidence against her!"

"*She* suggested Larkin Manor, as you'll remember," Carstairs said quickly.

"But you accepted an idea that was clearly irregular. Am I right?"

"It was a calculated gamble," Davis said.

"With my cousin's life. When she asked me to accept the Larkins' invitation, she said that she *was in a desperate state.* I thought that was hyperbole, because Poppy likes a bit of drama, but there was something more, wasn't there?"

I waited. The two inspectors traded glances. "She had apparently become uneasy about certain of Bosworth's activities, perhaps because of your warning," Davis said. "She took her concern to the major, her father's old friend. The major thought she was romancing but suggested the house party as an opportunity to find out. Not his best idea."

That was the first thing I could wholeheartedly agree on.

CHAPTER 6

Inspector Carstairs returned to Larkin Manor to direct the search parties. I returned to London with Inspector Davis, even though a third-class train ticket would have suited me better. "Expenses," he said drily and gave me to understand I was to be escorted. He focused on the road and drove in silence. Fine by me. Our meeting had left me with more questions than answers, and I had a lot to think about.

The one thing I understood was that Carstairs and Davis had different agendas. Carstairs wanted Freddie's killer. That Davis's brief was altogether more slippery and ill-defined was confirmed by his remarks when we arrived in London. "You'll have opportunities to be useful," he said, as if I was an anxious would-be volunteer.

I asked for details.

"Go about your usual routine but keep your eyes open," he said.

That did not seem much of a directive until he added, "Rinaldi."

"What about him?"

"You know him?"

"Only from this past weekend."

"A man you ought to meet again; I'll see it's arranged." He glanced at the sign above my showroom and checked the chairs, elegantly displayed in front of our distinctive white rubber drapes. "Very nice. You'll hear from me. Be sure to respond."

That sounded like a threat, but I didn't commit myself and went inside.

"Copper?" asked Nan, who had been watching from the window.

"Supposedly the Met."

She nodded. "The Met handles high-profile homicides." Nan's relish was muted only by my involvement and Poppy's. As soon as she heard the details, she declared that a visit to my aunt was essential. My idea of a telegram or a telephone call was off the table. "Besides," she said, "you'll need a list of Miss Poppy's closest friends. Examine her bedroom if you can. She'll have photos and maybe even letters. You'll perhaps learn who she trusts."

With this excellent advice in hand, I changed my shirt and socks, combed my hair, and set out for my aunt Theresa's, where drama ensued. My aunt is a social tiger and still quite a beauty. She was Deb of the Year back at the turn of the century, then a colonel's lady in the Punjab. As a result, she's struggled ever since the war with what she refers to as Modern Society. Capitalized. I was normally regarded as an Unregenerate Bohemian—please capitalize that as well—and I expected an uncomfortable and unproductive meeting.

My aunt met me with a wide-ranging denunciation of police, friends, and relatives. She was at her stormy best, but I saw that, underneath, she was frightened. This was not just about Modern Society but about her daughter, who irritates and disappoints her in some ways, but who is much loved and the last of her family.

"Aunt Theresa," I said when she caught her breath. "We need to find Poppy."

She came down to earth looking a couple decades older. "That Carstairs is supposedly searching," she said with a sniff. I guessed the laconic, smoke-embalmed Sussex inspector had not impressed. "Thank goodness, the Met is involved."

"And will be more involved now that Poppy's gone missing."

"They can't think she—" my aunt exclaimed, unable to finish the thought.

"Everyone who was at Larkin Manor's a possibility, but whoever planted that blouse did Poppy a favor, because now the police suspect that someone is trying to frame her. They hinted as much today. But they are troubled by her absence. Someone will undoubtedly be here fairly soon to question you and search her room."

This idea so irritated my aunt that she gave me the names of some of Poppy's friends—*featherheads every one, and two never came out properly*—before taking me up to her room. I feared that a thorough search under her eyes would be impossible, and I was wondering how best to proceed when my aunt was summoned for a telephone call.

I immediately opened the small writing desk and ruffled through Poppy's address book for the addresses and numbers of the *featherheads*, that is, friends known to my aunt, all from families with good incomes and correct pedigrees. Likely or even useful people to call if one was on the lam? I wasn't so sure.

Some letters awaiting answer were in the pigeonholes. They were bright with brittle deb chat but brief and as uninformative as the few cards saved from special formal dances and parties. Not a line indicated anyone Poppy would call in dire circumstances. Like my aunt, I was beginning to feel at sea with Modern Society, before I remembered Poppy's lonely bookshelf with her collection of schoolgirl scrapbooks and autograph albums. *Too juvenile for words* had been her assessment.

She was right about that. But Lizzie, who had pledged *undying friendship to my tough hockey cocaptain*, and Alexandra, who recalled *that orgy of Victoria cake* and *a certain boy from Eton*, raised my hopes. Especially the reference to the boy from Eton; I might have something in common with the deb set, after all. Lizzie's and Alexandra's surnames and addresses were in Poppy's book. If she remained missing, no doubt the police would work through the list and contact every one. I needed to be more selective.

I went through the drawers and closet again, neat and ship-shape, with all the garments we'd seen yesterday. Poppy had gone to Sussex with only the clothes on her back. She'd certainly want a change, especially if she had been out in last night's torrential storm. Provided, that was, that she was all right, that she was being reckless and indifferent to authority and not lying in some sodden field like Freddie.

No defeatism, Francis! She was fine, off somewhere with Lizzie or Alexandra, and I guessed that she'd avoid home, where her mother would have definite ideas about how to proceed, and head to the flat. I remembered that Poppy also kept the box with her contraceptive device there, another bit of Modern Society to be kept from Aunt Theresa's prying eyes. And what else? When we'd searched her rooms, we'd been looking for whatever Freddie might have hidden, not for letters or appointments to meet old friends. A visit to the flat was in order, and soon.

How to manage that? There was no helpful concierge. Assuming I could locate the landlord quickly, would I be able to talk my way in before Poppy's disappearance hit the press? Highly doubtful. I should have been instructed in the useful art of breaking and entering instead of Latin declensions and botanical phyla.

I stood still in the middle of the room. Thanks to my training with Maurice, I am strengthening an already good visual memory. *Think of yesterday, Francis. Imagine yesterday, searching this very room and giving it up as a bad job before Poppy offers a treat of tea and cake. She picks up her jacket from the bed, puts her hand in the right-hand pocket, and pulls out—keys. Yes, her now unneeded keys to the flat. Where did she put them? Concentrate!* I imagined her arm, shapely and muscular from riding, the elegant curve of her hand causing the rattle of metal on— on marble. I checked the fireplace mantel. The flat keys were safe in my pocket before Aunt Theresa returned along the hall.

I took the Tube to the British Museum and walked to Poppy's flat, where I trotted briskly up the stairs like a man absolutely entitled to be there. A quick look both ways down the hall, then I unlocked the door of the flat and slipped inside. "Poppy?" I called hopefully.

Silence. Of course, she wasn't there; Poppy was safe elsewhere. I drew the curtains and turned on the lights. Same drill: desk, drawers, closets, but this time looking for notes, letters. Freddie, I learned, had put his sentiments in writing. Absent his sapphire eyes, handsome shoulders, and muscular rump, even his prose seemed phony. *Forget Freddie!*

I was in the flat over an hour, and the closest I came to anything useful was a note in Poppy's writing: *Call Lizzie.* So, still very much in touch. A hockey cocaptain sounded like a girl who might be useful in a pickle. I'd call her first. I was ready to lock up when I noticed the small red leather box holding Poppy's Dutch cap, or whatever it was called. I'd been too much of a gentleman to open it while she was there, but now it couldn't hurt to satisfy my curiosity.

Inside was a simple, but rather alarming, rubber device. Could Freddie have been worth this? I closed the box and set it down. *Women are, indeed, the valiant sex*, I thought, and then I had another idea. I opened the box and removed the cap so that I could poke at what I'd registered as the slightly wrinkled lining. With the help of a nail file, I lifted the paper. Underneath were several dark strips: photo negatives. Freddie really was no gentleman.

Why hadn't he removed them after the quarrel? He'd stormed upstairs, leaving Poppy in the library. He could have gone into her room and collected the box. Something must have prevented him: chambermaid at work or that sly Rinaldi waiting in his room or the major eager to share some architectural tidbit? As a result, he'd left without what I suspected was his blackmail ammunition. Hence his return.

What now, Francis? Be a good citizen and inform Inspector Davis? I wasn't quite that civic-minded, especially when he'd demand to know how I'd gotten into the flat. Should I take the neutral course, put everything back, and leave the box for the police to discover? That would be safest for me, but I could already envision the headlines: SECRETS STASHED IN FORMER DEB'S FLAT, DEB'S UNMENTIONABLE HOLDS BLACKMAIL PHOTOS, SOCIETY GIRL'S SECRET LIFE. I pocketed the box, deciding there would be time enough to turn the negatives in after Poppy was found.

I switched off the lights and reopened the drapes in time to see a patrol car outside, the driver backing up and pulling ahead several times in a complicated maneuver to bring the vehicle to the curb. I stepped back from the window as they opened the car doors. Make a run downstairs, hide in the basement? Go up another floor and hope to loiter unobserved? Nonsense! Panic was absurd. I locked the door behind me and walked downstairs, trying to look discouraged and disconsolate— not terribly hard under the circumstances. Two uniformed cops were standing beside their patrol car, waiting for their superior. Inspector Davis, quite likely.

I was conscious of the leather box and Poppy's keys in my pocket, but I gave them a smile and a nod. One of them was worth a second look, too, with a heavy, rather rough face and wide shoulders. *Don't even think about that, Francis!*

"You live in this building, mate?" his partner asked. This one was thin, with scarred cheeks and a crooked nose, less enticing but clearly more savvy.

"I stopped by hoping to see a friend. But no luck." *Say nothing more, Francis!*

He nodded, and I walked off at a steady, good citizen pace until I turned the corner and spotted a bus arriving half a block away. I made it gasping just as the doors were closing. Two stops later, I was back on foot and making my way to the Tube, when I passed an available phone box. I tried both Lizzie of the hockey pitch and Alexandra, who favored boys from Eton. *Miss Elizabeth* was not available. The phone rang unanswered at Miss Alexandra's. I guessed that she lived on her own in a flat without a servant.

Could one or both of them be off somewhere with Poppy? That was my best hope, otherwise my cousin could be lying somewhere on the Downs. I shook my head at the thought. *Don't imagine disasters, Francis!* Poppy was quite capable negotiating the wretched countryside on her own and getting a ride back to London. Most likely, she was already at my aunt's. If so, she must stay there and not return to the flat that was even now crawling with coppers. I used my last pennies to call Aunt Theresa, but she'd had no word.

I didn't like that at all and to distract myself, I showed Nan the negatives as soon as I got home. "I just don't know what's on them."

"Why not let Ed develop them for you?"

Ed Winthrop owned a small photo shop nearby. He took my advertising photographs and recorded new designs, but I disliked involving him with the negatives. Dodgy photos had brought someone I knew in France to a nasty end, and I had a bad feeling about these. "I think I'd better know what's on them first."

"You'll need a strong light. And maybe my magnifying glass?"

I said that might do, and Nan fetched her large magnifier. I've noticed that she's using the glass more and more, and lately she's been complaining of how small the print is in her favorite newspapers. I don't like to think what that means.

I switched on my gooseneck desk lamp and squinted at the negatives. One strip, I thought, showed figures; the other seemed nothing more than a series of gray patterns. Neither was really legible until Nan brought the magnifying glass, and, when our fingers proved too awkward, a pair of tweezers. We turned the gooseneck lamp so that the bulb faced up. Nan held the film as steady as she could and, blinking from the glare, I moved the magnifying glass over the images, strange in their reversal of dark and light.

"Well!" said Nan.

Three naked men were entangled on a wash of black that must represent sheets. One's face was visible, the other two would have to be recognized by their bare nether anatomies. "Freddie Bosworth earned his money by keeping this sort of business secret," I said.

"Poor Miss Poppy!"

"Exactly."

"He was no gentleman, not taking and selling pictures like that," said Nan.

"I think that these photos are why he returned to Larkin Manor. And maybe why he was killed. Depending on who these men are."

"Are the photos all the same?"

"All men in motion, yes. But I can't tell if they're the same individuals. What about the other strip?"

She lifted the second one. "Blank, don't you think?"

"I doubt he'd have saved a damaged strip." I finally got the magnifying glass in the right place. "It's pages of a document, Nan."

"Can you make anything out?"

I pulled the magnifying glass back and moved it from side to side. "'*Chain*' something. That can't be right. '*Chain Home*.'"

"A funny name for a man."

"I'm not sure it's a man. There's something—I think the word is *magnetron*. Ever hear of such a thing?"

"Sounds like *magnet*. A scientific device? I don't think that's what those other pictures were about."

"Certainly not." I moved the glass back a little. "'*Bawdsey*' something '*Stat*—.' Maybe *Station*." I put down the glass and, blinking, Nan laid down the film. "I think Freddie branched out to some scientific material."

"Or used his old tricks to get new material," Nan suggested.

That seemed even more likely. I ran through the guests in my mind. Who would be more apt to buy such material than Rinaldi? No wonder he was in Freddie's room. "One of the guests was an Italian attaché or diplomat. Exact status unclear."

"Trust it to be some foreigner!" Nan exclaimed. "Killed him with a knife! And then he'd claim—what is it?"

"Diplomatic immunity. Could be." Especially since Inspector Davis was keen for me to meet Rinaldi again. "But before we do anything more, I'd better see if I can find out what a magnetron is."

At the British Museum reading room, I presented my question to a librarian. A consultation behind the desk followed. Finally, the fact that this was a piece of electromagnetic equipment was confirmed, and some proper citations obtained. I waited for two periodicals. One, in German that really stretched my Deutsch, discussed the work of an inventor named Christian Hülsmeyer. He'd obtained Reichspatent Nr. 165546 for a device to prevent ships colliding in fog.

Good and useful, I was sure, but my mysterious document was in English. Anyway, Hülsmeyer had not developed a magnetron, whatever that was, although he did work with mysterious waves, relatives of x-rays or radio waves. I turned with relief to the second, English language, journal. Highly technical, the article was mostly impenetrable, but in one paragraph, I came across *cavity magnetron*. On my fourth reading, I figured out that this hollow device caused streams of electrons to oscillate, producing something called microwaves.

Despite my best efforts, I understood little else, until I came to the conclusion of the article. The author noted that the device was useless as a radio amplifier but reported that these odd waves could be made to bounce off objects, thus revealing their position. But, I thought, Hülsmeyer had already found a way to protect ships. Hadn't Freddie known about that? Was I on a wild goose chase?

I sat tapping the desk. Certainly if the British navy had learned about Hülsmeyer's device, they would have jumped on it, so Freddie's document was undoubtedly out-of-date. For us, anyway. For the Italians? Possibly, but wouldn't they have read about the German's ingenious device for ships in fog? What else moved in fog? Trains, cars? Planes!

I returned the materials, thanked the librarian, and took the Tube straight home to question Nan, whose memory of the late war is both sharp and extensive.

"Dear boy, of course there was bombing!" she said. "Those damnable zeppelins came first, dumping bombs right and left wherever they wanted. Later on, it was planes, Gothas, mostly. They killed a lot of poor souls. Criminals was what they were, criminals. They just came out of nowhere, though whenever they could, our boys got up in the Sopwith Pups and Camels. I remember the first time a Camel crew shot down a bomber at night."

"High-risk work!"

"Bravest of the brave," said my nan. "You understand they could only fly in daytime or on moonlit nights. Otherwise they'd have been flying blind."

"And same for the gun crews on the ground trying to spot enemy bombers?"

"Of course."

"They needed a way to see in the dark," I said, thinking of Hülsmeyer's device for ships in fog.

"Might as well wish for Baron Munchausen's spectacles."

"I think that's what they're working on. I think that's maybe what Freddie got his hands on. We need to hide those negatives, Nan."

"Let me take care of that, dear boy." She wrapped them carefully in a piece of paper. "Who might come after them? Official or not?"

"Both, I'm afraid."

"Official needs a search warrant."

I nodded. "Whoever killed Freddie might not."

"Right. Then for now, behind that loose wallpaper in the alcove? I've been meaning to repaste the strip, anyway."

"Perfect," I said.

Nan hesitated for a moment. "I think in two different places," she said then. "They are really quite different."

"Right." My nan is big on classifications and on making distinctions. "Two separate places then. Who knows, we may have two different people after them."

CHAPTER 7

There was no sign of Poppy that night nor for the whole weekend. Aunt Theresa phoned the local vicar, her MP, the chief constables of two jurisdictions, and the editors of four major dailies without being any the wiser. Despite leaving several messages, I failed to connect to Poppy's friends, so the only things we learned that weekend were that the police were keeping an eye on Victoria Station arrivals and that no body had turned up on the Sussex Downs.

I would get discouraged, scared Poppy was dead, and minutes later I'd be furious that she'd taken French leave. The weekend was bad all around and concluded with a quarrel with Maurice, only partially redeemed by an exciting reconciliation. Normally, I quite like erotic drama, but under the circumstances, even his studio paled. Monday night, I phoned to say I had some last-minute designs to finish up. True enough, but what I actually did was shine my shoes, darken up my hair, and set off for Piccadilly Circus, home to the Dilly Boys, working-class chaps out for an evening and willing to give well-heeled gents a good time.

Why did I do that—other than the obvious? A subconscious

agenda, Maurice would say. He knows all about Freud and has been educating me on the subconscious and hidden drives—and not so hidden ones, too. He says that our ideas are not all under our control (no surprise there) and that ideas for paintings really spring from unconscious impulses. That night, I must have had an idea percolating, because I turned down a good-looking boy and a burly fellow who would have suited me fine and fattened my purse. Such restraint was rewarded when I was passing under the giant lighted Bovril sign. Just ahead was a well-set-up fellow in a short jacket. Underneath, I recognized the muscular rump last seen in knee breeches. Monday was the agreeable Jenkins's night off, and I remembered that he usually spent it in London.

"Hello, Jenkins!"

He turned and, I thought, hesitated just a beat before he smiled. "Hello, Mr. Bacon."

"On the Dilly, it's plain Francis."

"Not Francine?" When he winked, I knew things would go all right. We had beer and sandwiches and got on so well that I nixed the idea of a hotel room. Back we went to the design studio, and after various amusements, he became forthcoming about Larkin Manor.

"I'm worried sick about Poppy," I said. "She was bruised to a fare-thee-well. I can't imagine she was in any shape to walk miles on a wet night. She could be dead and buried on the Downs for all we know."

"Miss Penelope," Jenkins said carefully, "was assisted."

I sat up in bed. "Assisted? You mean in leaving the manor?"

"The major thought it best she left."

Well! Magnus Larkin was a much better actor than I'd cred-
ited. I'd quite believed he was as surprised as the rest of us. "Do
you know why?"

"Mysterious are the ways of the officer corps. I think he felt
unable to protect her. But same old, same old. He gives an order
and expects it to be carried out."

"He was your officer in the war," I guessed.

"That's right. I was his batman, and he was better than most.
After the war, I needed a job." He paused a moment. "And even
though he couldn't really afford me, I think the major wanted a
familiar face."

I wondered who could be more familiar than his wife and
daughter.

Jenkins didn't answer for a moment. He found his cigarettes
and lit one. Smokers always have an excuse to delay an answer or
to marshal their thoughts. I may take to carrying fags about just
to be able to fiddle with the packet. "The western front," he said
finally, "was another world, and ever since, we've been citizens elsewhere. It's not a place we can talk about with the people at home."

I nodded. I'd met other soldiers with the same reaction. "You
took Poppy somewhere?"

"I drove her to Hastings very late to the big convalescent
home the major knew and dropped her off. It's where the major
recovered after the war, so he knows the staff. I told her that she'd
be safe there and to stay put."

"But she didn't."

"Too right. I was sent out again yesterday afternoon. I was
supposed to pick her up, *cover her tracks*, as the major said, but

Miss Penelope had already made another arrangement. According to the convalescent home, she'd gone that very morning."

I thought this over and felt better in one way, worse in another. Poppy hadn't met Freddie's fate at Larkin Manor, but she was still missing and could not be assumed safe. She must have had a very good reason to drop out of sight with no word to anyone, not even her mother. "Did you have guests this past weekend?"

"The Tollmans stayed the weekend, and the Groves came for Sunday lunch. They're pretty much a fixture lately." His cigarette glowed red as he drew in the smoke. "The madame is very interested in politics."

"And the major?"

"He'd like to see all politicians shot," said Jenkins.

The next day, I saw Jenkins off to an early train and got right to my drawing desk where I was busy all morning with pencils and watercolors. I finished up the designs I had promised, and by two o'clock, weary of virtue, I decided I deserved a break. I was putting on my jacket when the bell rang in the showroom. There was Signor Rinaldi, another visitor from Larkin Manor. Could that be a coincidence?

"*Buongiorno*, Signor Rinaldi," I said. My Italian, such as it is, was mostly learned from cheap London eateries.

"Ah, Mr. Bacon," he replied and bowed. Today, he was a courtly item, all charm and flourishes. "I have come to visit the delightful studio that I have heard so much about." And he beamed.

I thought it best to go into my usual spiel, that we offered the latest in Continental design, adapted for the English market and fabricated locally. "Good British construction," I concluded, although most of my workmen were German Jewish exiles.

He went over to the small display rugs and petted them like dogs, a reason I try to put light-colored rugs out of reach. "Furniture, too," he remarked. "Impressive. The major had mentioned your work, but as so many of your nation are amateurs, I did not expect this."

I smiled at his condescension; I personally thought Italy's great artistic days were behind it—no matter what Mussolini said.

"We did not have a chance to talk at the manor, not after that most distressing event! And the fair Miss Penelope?"

I shook my head. "No word."

"The methods of the English police are different," he said. His haughty expression suggested how much more satisfactory the results would be in Il Duce's Rome.

I did not respond, but Signor Rinaldi was not to be discouraged. He suggested that we might have a drink to remember poor Freddie, whom we had known as the others had not. I was a trifle surprised; previously Rinaldi had seemed as indifferent to Freddie's fate as the others at the house party.

"I was just going to lunch," I said, "but I could manage a drink."

Rinaldi became enthusiastic. He knew a very good Italian restaurant in Soho with the most excellent fish and proper wines. "Not the usual exports. You will enjoy," he assured me and led the way to Taverna Firenze. It was an upscale restaurant with paneled wainscoting, ornately patterned wallpapers, and a small army of allegorical nudes. I believe that we were seated under Wisdom, an ironic choice for us, but the service was princely, and the food was so good that I began to see the point of diplomacy. The wine, too, was marvelous, and with our second glass, Rinaldi proposed a toast to Freddie.

I raised my glass with many reservations. "To a man of the future!" Rinaldi said, and he repeated the phrase in his native language.

"I would have said Freddie was a man of the past," I ventured. "He had the traditional ambition of marrying an heiress."

"No, no," Rinaldi said. "He belonged to the future. He saw the wave of history."

More like its backside, I thought.

"He understood the necessity for change, for consolidation, for a strong central director."

"For someone like your Mussolini?"

"Il Duce has restored Italy to a greatness not seen since the Romans."

"I don't know about that. After all, the sun never sets on the British Empire."

Rinaldi waved this off. "Your empire has passed its peak. The future is with the new men of the new order, men with strength and discipline."

"That doesn't sound much like the Freddie I knew."

"Nonetheless, Freddie served the future."

"Really?"

"He was a patriot, eager to promote ideas his own country lacked. He felt a resurgent Italy would rouse the sleeping British lion," Rinaldi concluded and showed me his perfect teeth.

A most ingenious defense of selling out one's country! I

wondered if Freddie had believed any such thing. "I am surprised, Signor Rinaldi. You probably don't know his reputation
here, but the rumor was that his lovers were lucky to escape with
reputations intact and wallets only half empty."

Rinaldi's toothy grin vanished. He leaned forward, all business. "Great empires are built on great—and little—crimes. One
must be willing to dirty, even bloody, one's hands."

"Someone felt that way at the manor."

Rinaldi shrugged; his gestures struck me as more eloquent
than his speech. "Freddie, as you say, had bad habits. Lately,
politically enlightened, he put them to better use."

"Really?"

Signor Rinaldi nodded vigorously. "Look at England now.
Unemployment, want, dissension, yes? Misery and poverty in
the north, the homeless on the Embankment, ragged children
in the streets. This country needs a firm hand and a planned,
rational economy."

"Plus a big military?" I asked, remembering Il Duce's recent
military ventures.

"A great nation needs a great army," he said. "It absorbs the
jobless and gives direction to the aimless."

"I still do not see where Freddie fits in. He detested honest
work, and his whole aim was money."

Signor Rinaldi looked around and dropped his voice. "Freddie found useful information for me. He sometimes uncovered
things such as are good for diplomats to know."

I'll bet, I thought.

"Before the Larkins' house party, he indicated that he had

something important for me, but he wanted more money than usual. We were in negotiations about the price when the fatal quarrel with the fair Miss Penelope occurred."

"Bad timing from your point of view," I agreed.

"But now I have hopes."

"Really?"

"Let us not play about, Mr. Bacon." Rinaldi's voice sharpened. "Freddie claimed to have the material with him, but I never saw it. I assume he hid it somewhere at Larkin Manor. Why else would he have returned after such a dramatic exit?"

"Agreed, but why not take it with him in the first place?"

"He did not have the opportunity, suggesting that he must have hidden it somewhere outside his own room."

"And you believe this because—"

"Because I searched his room—but only his room. Whereas you and the divine Miss Penelope had ample opportunity to search her possessions."

"What makes you think we'd have thought of such a thing?"

"Do not pretend to be stupid. You were both observed. Right up until your cousin disappeared."

That, I thought, explained the mystery man lurking outside Poppy's mother's house and probably the chap on the motorbike, too. "Poppy was nervous about her flat," I said. I find it is best when lying to include as much of the truth as possible. "She sensed that someone had been in the flat and she wanted me to go with her."

"Yet you returned alone to the flat just the other day. Suggesting you must have a key."

"Not at all," I said, although I was alarmed: I'd been sure the only people who noticed me were the two cops in the patrol car. "I went on the off chance Poppy had returned. The front door was unlocked, but she wasn't there, and I wasn't able to get into her flat."

"So unfortunate," Rinaldi said. "Freddie believed his information was worth a hundred pounds. A useful sum for any young man."

"A sum that would tempt me if I had found anything. Of course, once you had the information in hand, there is no guarantee you would think it worth so much."

"There's risk for both sides in these negotiations," Rinaldi said in a philosophical tone, and he signaled the waiter. "We will finish with grappa. You've had grappa?"

I shook my head.

"You must try grappa! A very special drink." He added something in rapid Italian to the waiter.

I wasn't paying much attention. I was trying to recall the exact appearance of the street outside Poppy's apartment. I could only remember seeing a few passing cars and two or three women occupied with shopping bags before the arrival of the police car. No suspicious loiterers. No men on motorbikes. No men, at all, along the quiet street. That left only the two cops, an idea that made me anxious. What if one of them—or their officer—was somehow in touch with Rinaldi? What would that mean?

Two small glasses arrived with a clear liquid just touched with gold. The waiter set them down with ceremonious care.

"*Salute*," said Rinaldi.

"Cheers!" I took a sip. It was potent and a little bit odd, but I

drank it up. Almost immediately the room began to waver, causing Rinaldi to lose definition in an interesting way, as if his flesh
were melting and shifting to take on new forms.

"You've drugged me," I said. Or thought I said, for I am
uncertain that my vocal apparatus was working. While I have a
good head for alcohol, drugs affect me too strongly and quickly
to give me any pleasure. I stood up. Or thought I did, but maybe
I was not successful, for the last things I saw before I was lifted
into utter darkness was the tiled floor and a leg of the table.

Rustling nearby. Rats in the old stable? Mice in the kitchen walls?
Walls where a bus was heaving itself into gear? I opened my eyes
on darkness and then on wavering lights that combined with
the smell of fuel and garbage to stir my digestive system. With
my head throbbing and acid filling my mouth, I levered myself
upon one elbow and lost the best meal I'd had since I returned
to England. I wiped my face on my handkerchief. I was looking
at a high wall. And bins. There appeared to be a deal of elderly
vegetables in the neighborhood, probably keeping company with
rancid fat.

I shifted my legs, happy to feel them move, and caught my
knee on something sharp. I shifted the other way and my elbow
connected with something splintery. A little more investigation
showed that I was lying on a heap of splintered wooden crates.
That suggested an alley. Near a market or restaurants. I staggered
to my feet, the walls on either side wobbling. I leaned against the
bricks and moved toward a rectangle of night sky and unstable
lighting.

Ahead of me was a park, and as my head cleared somewhat, I recognized Soho Square. With its streetlights on. So it was evening. When I'd last been on planet Earth, it had been afternoon, and I'd been sitting under Minerva, goddess of wisdom, being foolish with . . . with Rinaldi. I remembered that I'd denied having anything of Freddie's but hadn't absolutely closed the door. *Bad move, Francis.*

Maybe it wouldn't have mattered, not if Rinaldi knew I'd been at Poppy's and her mother's. He might even think we'd found the material earlier. In fact, he must have, if he was, as I now suspected, behind the purse snatching that broke Poppy's arm. Did that clear the men in the squad car? Would I be safest to put those negatives into Inspector Davis's eager hands? In my present state, I wasn't sure. Poppy had been watched and attacked in the hopes of getting them. Then nothing. I find the negatives and, voilà, I'm taken out to lunch with Rinaldi, who—

What precisely had he done? I patted my pockets. My keys were gone; fortunately I had not been carrying Pops's with me. Money? I patted my pockets. I still had three shillings and seven pence, but the lining of the little change purse had been slit, so a careful search. Rinaldi and his associates—he couldn't be acting alone—were serious; they'd gotten an elegant restaurant to drug a patron and managed to get me out of the dining room and off to Soho Square with a search in between.

Slick moves, but I thought they'd given up rather too easily. I was convinced I had been unconscious almost from the moment I hit the floor. Their search turned up nothing. I wasn't carrying whatever they'd expected from Freddie. Wouldn't they have been

tempted to let me regain my senses and then beat the information out of me?

Or was that too compromising for the fancy eatery? Maybe,
but I suspected Mussolini's boys could get away with a lot, even
in London where the immigrant population had folks back home
in the new Italy to worry about. Were they convinced I was tell-
ing the truth? I doubted that very much. I stuck my hand in my
pocket, meaning to rattle my keys, a habit Nan deplores, even
though I already knew my keys were gone. This time, though,
the loss registered. I'd been spared a beating or worse because
they thought they had what they needed.

I had to warn Nan. I had to get back to the studio. I started
to run across the square, swayed, almost fell, caught myself, and
cautious although my heart was jumping, started walking, and
running whenever I was able, back to the studio.

CHAPTER 8

I staggered toward Avant Design, bouncing off lampposts and pillar boxes with my heart jumping and my lungs protesting. The door showed the Closed sign, just as I'd left it: I'd arrived in time; I'd panicked unnecessarily; all was well. I fumbled for my keys, remembered they were lost, and began pounding on the door. "Nan! Nan! It's me!"

No answer. They had come, Nan was hurt, maybe even—I hit the door with all my strength, rattled the handle, and almost fell facedown when the unlocked door swung open. "Nan!"

Inside the showroom, the sample rugs had been torn from the walls, the leather backs and seats on the two display chairs, slashed. I opened the door to the back. Broken crockery lay on the kitchen floor, and papers and finished designs were strewn about my studio, along with the contents of the upturned drawers of my worktable. "Nan!"

A sound from my bedroom. I found her lying across the bed, gagged with hands and feet tied, looking very small, white, and fragile. When I was a child, Nan had been my protector, the one person I could rely on, and she'd always seemed large and power-ful. I realized with a shock that had been a trick of perspective, an illusion created to protect and encourage me. I untied the rag across her mouth. "Are you hurt? Are you hurt, Nan?"

She shook her head. I struggled to unpick the knots before lurching off to get my scissors to cut the ropes.

Freed, she sat up, rubbing her wrists. "Just bumps and bruises. Nothing to write home about." She looked through to the show-room. "Oh, your lovely chairs! Dear boy! I am so sorry. I must not have locked the door when you left."

"No, no, Nan, they had a key. They stole mine."

"That's why I heard the rattle of the lock and thought you were back. I went through to say hello and there they were. Two big fellows with cloth caps pulled down. And wearing gloves. I wondered why."

I pressed her hand.

"I told them that they'd have to come back later, that the studio was closed for lunch, and they said they'd come for Fred-die's stuff."

"That's how they put it? Not photographs or papers?"

Nan thought for a minute. "No, that's odd, isn't it? I think they weren't quite sure what they were looking for."

"Or what form it was in?"

"That must be it. They went through your desk, I know they did. I told them to see they put everything back, and they told me to get out of the room. I thought I could get to the front door. That's when they tied me up. They didn't get Miss Poppy's key, though. You'd left it in the kitchen, and I'd slipped it into my pocket." She held it up.

"Good show, Nan!"

"I was so worried you'd come back while they were here, Francis, and then I was afraid something had happened to you, when you were so late. It is late, isn't it? They'd pulled the shades down, but I could tell the light was going."

I sat beside her and told her about my lunch with Rinaldi, concluding with our little glasses of grappa.

"Grappa? One of those Italian drinks?" My nan is staunch for all things British.

"It tasted odd, but I thought that's what grappa tasted like."

"Most likely! Another of those queer foreign things."

"Right, but with something distinctly off in it. I came to in Soho Square. Money in my pocket but no keys."

"Dear boy! You were shanghaied."

"The closest I'll get to being a sailor. But, Nan, the negatives. Did they find the negatives?"

"Certainly not, though I expected any minute they'd start on the walls. But they didn't." She sniffed. "Maybe not really skilled labor?"

"Lucky for us."

"But your chairs, your nice sketches! And the rugs. Are the rugs all right?"

"The main thing is that you are all right, Nan! If the chair frames are intact, the seats and backs can be replaced. I don't know about the rugs. I'll have a look."

Now that Nan was safe, I could be upset about the show-room. The rugs had small tears where they had been carelessly pulled from the hooks, but the intruders hadn't thought to slash the backing, and Nan could probably mend them. The chair frames were fine; the good leather seats, backs, and arm covers would all need replacement. Money out the door.

In my workroom, pens, brushes, pencils, paints, and supplies had been dumped on the floor and finished drawings trampled underfoot. Although many were torn, I saw that I could salvage some work: This time, our intruders had been on a search, rather than destroy, mission. Next time, we might not be so lucky. I wedged the stoutest chair in the house under the front doorknob and told Nan we would have to call a locksmith.

"The police, too, dear boy. For your insurance claim."

I hate contacting the police for any reason, but she was right. Not to call them, especially if Rinaldi had a contact at the Met, would suggest we had something to hide. The only question was what to tell them, and I thought that over while Nan made us a nursery supper of toast and hard-boiled eggs, washed down with a lot of strong tea with sugar. After we finished eating, and before I could come up with an excuse, I nipped around to the corner phone box and dialed Inspector Davis's number.

To my surprise, he answered. Give the man credit, he worked long hours. "You wanted me to see more of Rinaldi," I said. "I've now seen too much of him. He drugged me at lunch, stole my keys, and sent two men to terrorize Nan. They ripped up my design studio. I'm going to have to file an insurance claim."

"We'll talk in person," Davis said, rather quickly, I thought, and promised to stop by that night. He arrived within the hour, accompanied by a slim, dark sergeant who was delegated to take Nan's statement. The sergeant had liquid black eyes and an insinuating manner that made me wonder if sergeants were chiefly selected to contrast with their leaders.

"Who knows how long I'd have lain there if my dear boy hadn't come back," Nan said. "We've touched nothing, except the crockery. We had to shift that. They left broken china all over the kitchen floor."

"Looking for something, were they?"

"Must have been," she said with a straight face. "Though I told them we hadn't a bean except for the studio samples."

When Nan took the sergeant through to the back rooms to see the other damage, Davis gave me a sour look. "You handled that badly," he said.

That was rich! "Signor Rinaldi stopped by the studio," I said, struggling with my temper. "I was just leaving for lunch, and he invited me to the Taverna Firenze."

"Nice to be on a diplomat's expenses."

"Very nice. I can recommend everything except the grappa. Mine was drugged." I described coming to amid a pile of crates off Soho Square without my keys. "I could barely walk."

Inspector Davis looked skeptical. "Why would an Italian attaché do that?"

Here was the delicate moment. I needed to convince him—as I hoped the futile search had convinced Rinaldi—that I had nothing of value. "He labors under the impression that I'd found whatever it was Freddie wanted to sell him. He offered me a hundred pounds. Money I certainly could use now." I nodded toward the damaged chairs.

Inspector Davis was silent for a moment. A hundred pounds

was a significant sum. "So Bosworth had been selling information to the Italians?"

"From what Rinaldi implied, they had an ongoing arrangement."

"Bosworth's normal line was compromising photographs of the rich and influential."

"Possibly he branched out, but I haven't a clue what he did with the material. As I've already told you, there was nothing out of place when Poppy and I visited her flat, no mysterious documents or surprise packages, nothing."

I waited for him to ask if I'd visited Poppy's flat again. That would be the natural question, but he didn't raise the subject. Was he convinced of my innocence? Or did he already know I'd been seen leaving the building? And if he didn't know, did that mean one of his patrolmen was Rinaldi's contact? Questions, questions! As I told Nan later, there were plenty of possibilities, and all of them were bad.

She still leaned toward trusting the Met, whose exploits she followed in the *Telegraph*'s crime news. "You can't be absolutely sure no one but the two policemen saw you near Miss Poppy's flat."

"No, I can't. But I'm sure enough that I don't want to take a chance. Freddie was killed, Poppy's still missing, I was drugged, and you were threatened. If one of those cops is dirty, what's to keep us safe after we hand over the negatives?"

Nan took this under advisement. At last she said, "Only one thing to do. You'll have to contact your uncle."

"Lastings is an unregenerate rogue."

"Of course, he is, dear boy, but he's British through and

through. He'll not let anything valuable fall into the hands of that fat Italian rascal Mussolini."

There was something to that, but ever since my uncle removed some dodgy paintings he'd been storing at my studio, he'd made himself scarce. We hadn't parted on the best of terms, either. "I haven't seen Uncle Lastings in months. He could be off, you know, being someone else. For all I know, he's decided to become a Frenchman again." Being temporarily French had been an integral part of a recent scheme to solicit genuine portraits of a bogus actress, a typical Lastings maneuver.

"I don't see you have another choice," she said.

I argued this for a while, but eventually, I agreed to try contacting him. "Sometime. But those films can't harm anyone as long as they're in our hands."

Nan agreed this was very true, but I could tell she was unenthusiastic about the delay. "I feel we should do something," she said. "Miss Poppy, now. Where is she? Why hasn't she been found? You need to talk to your aunt again. I think you should go down to Hastings and see that Inspector Carstairs."

The mention of Aunt Theresa made me think I'd almost rather deal with Uncle Lastings. As far as relatives went, I was between Scylla and Charybdis.

I was still undecided which was the lesser evil when Nan brought me the mail the next morning. Second from the bottom was a pale blue envelope with my address in a bold feminine hand. There was a faint hint of perfume, too.

"Well?" said Nan and raised her eyebrows.

"Perhaps Avant Design has a secret admirer." But I was wrong. Inside was a brief note in the same distinctive hand. *Call me soonest. Poppy's disappeared for real. She said to trust you.* It was signed *Elizabeth Armitage.* I handed the note to Nan.

"Sounds as if they'd been in touch and now Miss Poppy has vanished."

"It does sound like it," I agreed.

"Don't wait around, dear boy. I can handle the insurance adjuster. And shall I write to that Mr. Mendelssohn? About repairing the chairs?"

"Yes, but tell him it will be a week or so before I can bring them," I said as I headed to the phone box. The servant who answered my call went to find *Miss Elizabeth.* "This is Francis, Poppy's cousin," I said when she came on the line.

Immediately, her voice changed, undoubtedly for someone else's benefit. "Oh, Edwina! How terrific to hear from you. Of course, we can get together! Too fun! Early lunch at a Lyons?"

I agreed, and she selected a Corner House within walking distance. "Twenty minutes," she said and hung up.

At the Lyons, I was lucky to find a seat near the door where I could watch new arrivals. A slim, dark woman looked too fashionable for the ex-hockey captain, and she started waving to friends the minute she crossed the threshold. Three girls together, arm in arm, giggling through the door, were all equally unlikely. Several matrons, too old by a decade, arrived, loaded with shopping, before a solidly constructed blonde with a short, sensible haircut, a rose twin set, a tweed skirt, and an athlete's muscular swagger appeared. I stood up, and she immediately came to the table and sat down.

"Francis. Supposedly, Pops's cousin." No smile on her wide face, no greeting, all business.

"Her mother would vouch for me," I said, "but I don't think you want to involve Aunt Theresa." Then I had an inspiration. I pulled out my wallet and handed her my ticket for the British Museum's Reading Room. "Will that do?"

"You're Francis, all right." She returned the card. "Poppy said you're a real intellectual."

"You've heard from her?"

Just then, a Nippy, smart in her black outfit with starched white collar, cuffs, and apron, came to take our order.

"Tea and sandwiches do you, Francis?" Lizzie asked.

I said that would be fine and waited on pins and needles, as Nan would say, before the waitress disappeared with our order and Lizzie nodded. "She called me from Hastings."

"When?"

"The first call came the day that her disappearance hit the papers. I'd just been reading the story when the phone rang. Thank goodness Nell didn't recognize the voice."

"And Poppy was safe then?"

"She thought so. At that moment, anyway. I wanted to phone her mother, I thought I ought to, but Pops about blew her top. She had to stay away, because her mother would have the police and press and everyone down on her."

"She might have done. What a mess! The constabulary started searching the morning she was gone. Poppy'll be up for wasting police time."

"Minor detail," Lizzie said. "Here come our sandwiches."

"If that's minor, what's major?"

"Eat," said Lizzie, "then let's take a walk."

I was certainly getting a different view of debs and hockey players. Lizzie said nothing more to the point until we'd finished off the cheese, tomato, and cucumber sandwiches and emptied our pot of tea, giving me plenty of time to study her strong, even features. Personally, as far as subjects go, I prefer a few oddities in a face, but I had to admit that Poppy's athletic friend showed what Nan would call an abundance of character.

Outside the Lyons, she looked both ways, took my arm, and set a course for Russell Square. "Poppy doesn't trust the police," she said.

"Normally, I'd be the first to agree, but in this case . . ."

Lizzie shook her head. "This case especially. I don't know the ins and outs, but Pops seemed really frightened. First time ever, I'm guessing."

"She did find Freddie's corpse."

"This isn't about Freddie's death. She's taken that pretty calmly. It's whatever she learned about Freddie."

I thought that over. Although she'd been shattered by the discovery of Freddie's corpse, she'd recovered well. Or seemed to. And then there was the desperate summons to Larkin Manor to be considered. "Poppy sounded distraught when she asked me to the house party, though when I arrived, she seemed the same as ever."

"She was very good in the *Mikado* at school."

That struck me as a non sequitur until she added, "She played the Lord High Executioner," and gave me a puckish smile.

"My cousin has hidden talents."

"Too right. And I think—" Lizzie paused and said no more until we reached the square and started along one of the curving paths under the trees. Then she stopped in the middle of the path, as if uncertain what, or how much, to say. "Her late father was military intelligence. I guess you knew that." A questioning look.

"I only knew that he was a colonel in India."

"He had contacts," Lizzie continued. "Pops knows at least some of them. I think she discovered something and told one of them and landed herself in a mess."

"Maybe right before the Larkin house party?"

"Possibly. Was there any other reason to invite you? I don't mean that rudely."

"Understood. Poppy knew I hated the country and country house parties. The note she sent me wasn't like her at all."

"She didn't sound like herself with me, either. We need to find her, Francis, and make sure she's safe."

"You said that she called you more than once. Did she give you a phone number?"

"Yes, a Hastings number and a time to call, which I thought was odd, but it turned out to be a public phone box."

"And you tried to call her back?"

"At the time suggested. A passerby finally answered. The phone box was on the seafront. I could hear gulls and music. Since then, nothing at all. Now I'm thinking I should break my word and contact the police."

"Maybe. Inspector Carstairs, the local chap, seems fine. The guy from the Met, I'm not so sure about. But I should have told you straightaway that the autopsy report has changed the situation. Anyone at the manor—or indeed the passing stranger—could have murdered Freddie, because he had already been disabled by a fall before his throat was slashed. That's bad for Poppy. What's good is that someone appears to be trying to implicate her, and the police have picked up on that. For what it's worth, I think she's been moved down on the suspect list."

Lizzie seemed both unsurprised—such faith in my cousin!—and nonchalant—consorting with a potential murder suspect! All she said was, "Could you go down to Sussex with me tomorrow?"

I thought of my damaged studio, the bills for the locksmith, and the repair of my sample chairs, not to mention the probable delays of the insurance, and said, "I could about manage a third-class return."

"I'll borrow my brother's car. That way we can easily get down and back before dark, and we'll be able to cover more ground than on foot or by public transport."

She seemed so competent, I wondered why she wanted my company, but I said that was a capital idea.

"I'll maybe have to work on George for a bit, so call me tonight just to be sure we're on. Any time after nine, but don't give your own name again. It was just lucky Nell picked up. She's hard of hearing. Mother hears too much, and she reads all the news stories. If she answers, she'll know what I'm about, and there'll be a fine to-do. Be Tony. Do you like 'Tony'?"

More spy novel stuff. I thought I'd left all that behind on the Continent. "Tony's fine, but I rather fancied Edwina."

"Let's give my mother hope," she said and winked.

Ah, so she was a female member of my tribe, complete with anxious and disapproving parents. We exchanged a look of complete understanding before she leaned over, kissed my cheek, and strode away.

CHAPTER 9

The next morning, just after seven, a bright red saloon with a black top pulled up outside Avant Design. I hopped in. The leather interior smelled like a tack room and the dashboard and fittings were burl maple. The ride was as smooth as a sofa, and when we left the city, Lizzie pushed the speed up over 50 mph.

"Impressive," I said.

"A Morris 8 saloon with lots of custom touches. George's baby. I had to promise him the earth to get a loan."

"George is your older brother?"

"That's right. Next in line for the firm. But when Daddy retires, I'll have to take over the business end. George can do anything with math so long as it doesn't involve money."

"What does the company do?" I asked, just to keep the conversation going.

"Armitage, Ltd., makes electrical equipment, switches, relays, transformers."

"Very forward looking."

"Absolutely," Lizzie said, "and George is in the forefront."

"Really?"

"He's a genius engineer but otherwise a dolt. Did you know he introduced Pops to Freddie? The fatal man, gorgeous but toxic—not that George would have noticed. The only things he notices under the hood, so to speak, are motors."

You can bet that gave me something to think about: a genius electrical engineer who knew Freddie! Did George know about mysterious waves and magnetrons? Had I worried about all the wrong people? These were unpleasant thoughts under the circumstances, and I think the trip would have become awkward if Lizzie hadn't clearly enjoyed driving. Rolling along, she told me amusing stories about her schooldays with Poppy. I equate school with penal servitude, but she recalled their establishment as a jolly place where they played rough games on the hockey pitch and toasted bread and sausages in their rooms and made eyes at suitable boys. "Or girls," Lizzie added and winked.

"Would Poppy have stuck to girls! Or at least not picked such a rascal."

"Damn handsome just the same," Lizzie said, and I wondered how much she knew about the late Freddie. But though I tried several times to steer the conversation back to him, Lizzie offered nothing more. Something to think about there, too.

We turned onto the Grand Parade in Hastings at midmorning. The summer holiday makers had departed, but a good number of truants, lovers, convalescents, and ancients were out on the seafront enjoying the mild weather, the clouded sun, those supposedly healthy sea breezes. I'm not fond of the sea. Although sandy resorts are a big step up from country living, they're still a big step down from London and civilized life.

"We used to go to the pier when I was a child," Lizzie said, nodding toward the cluster of bulbous pleasure domes perched at the end of a long pier. "We'll go, if we have time."

The joys of dancing and other recreations while perched over many feet of salt water escape me completely, but I said, "If we can find Poppy, I'll be happy to go."

She gave me a glance as if she'd read my mind. "You're very fond of Pops, aren't you?"

"My favorite relative, hands down."

Lizzie glanced up at the rows of five- and six-story hotels facing the front and said, "We need a plan of attack."

That would have been the moment for me to mention the convalescent home, the big one that was so busy during the war, but I didn't. Maurice would say my subconscious was sending me warnings. "What we have is a phone box on the front," I said. "Maybe find that first and narrow down the search?"

"I can't think of anything better," she said.

We left George's saloon in the fine new car park and walked to the seafront, arriving quite near the Queen's Hotel, a big whipped cream–colored building with balconies and a fancy porte cochere where expensive cars were discharging well-heeled guests: Poppy's normal sort of place.

"What do you think of that?" Lizzie asked.

I shrugged. "She'd need a suitcase and dry clothes, but there are shops aplenty, so she'd have gotten a room. Big hotels have security, too, and people around all the time."

"So safer in one way. But her photo has been in the papers. What do you think the chances are of someone recognizing her?"

"Not too many can afford luxury digs at the moment, and they're mostly in the same set. So pretty good unless she kept to her room."

"That I don't see."

I agreed. My cousin was not the sort to cower in any hotel room, no matter how luxurious. I nodded toward a phone box on the other side of the street. "Shall we start with that one?"

Over on the beach side, people strolled the sidewalk above the sand, sat on the benches, or leaned against the railings, braving the brisk wind to stare at the sea. It stared back, gray-green, turbulent, and potentially hostile. Farther down the shore, the pier ventured out on its high iron legs like some queer insect, and faint sounds of music drifted from the pavilions. Lizzie went one way and I went the other, checking the numbers of the phones in the public kiosks. I was bored with sea air and getting discouraged when I saw her waving far down the street.

When I arrived at the kiosk, Lizzie held up the scrap of paper with the phone number. "She was here! Three days ago. Right here!"

We were still in the resort belt with terraced housing and cheek-by-jowl detached homes, all big and solid and most sporting B&B or hotel signs. Farther along, the ground rose abruptly. The buildings of the town slid away while the steep, green hills of the Downs occupied the horizon and overlooked the sea.

We split up again to visit establishments along this promising section of the front. I don't know what story Lizzie invented, but I was looking for a cousin who'd suffered a breakdown following the death of her fiancé. She'd been on a recuperative holiday but dropped out of contact after a couple penny postcards from Hastings and a single phone call. I thought my spiel both convincing and touching, but I got no response. Only one hotel manager had any reaction at all, a touch of evasiveness that was as likely due to indigestion or a difficult guest as to anything significant.

I rested my hopes on Lizzie, but she came up empty, too. By then, the light was dropping behind the hills, and she'd promised to return the car before dark. "Won't happen even if we leave now," she admitted.

I walked back with her, but near the car park, I abruptly changed my mind. "I think I should stay overnight. If Poppy is lying low here, she might chance a restaurant in the evening. She might even fancy a walk along the front. I'll catch a train in the morning—could you let Nan know?"

"Of course. I think there's an old kit bag in the boot of the car. You'll need a bag to take a room."

Actually, I'd had other plans for obtaining lodgings, anticipating a troll along the promenade or around the better restaurants and cinemas to pick up a well-heeled visitor. I could fancy a fine room with elegant room service. I like eating in bed—and I like chilled Champagne and chocolate biscuits. The weakness of my plan was that it left everything to a chance encounter and a complacent hotel deskman, while sober respectability could secure me a room in our target area. Not without some regret, I told Lizzie, "Good idea."

An hour later, I was occupying a second-floor room with a sea view very close to the phone box Poppy had used. I sat at the window for a while, keeping watch along the beachfront walk and the entrances to the various B&Bs and hotels until the sun set and the streetlights came on. Then I smoothed my hair and sallied out for the evening, still hoping for an elegant dinner at someone else's expense.

Fortune decided otherwise. Despite starting early and wandering late, I wound up sharing meat pies and beer with a fisherman, one of the fleet whose boats were beached nightly on the shingle. Ernie was thin and angular with strong, if asymmetric, features, the result, he said, of a boom catching the side of his face. His skin was as dark and leathery as a man twice his age and his light eyes seemed at once distant and sly. He divided up the pies with a lethal-looking fish knife, and on closer acquaintance, he carried a perfume of fish, salt, and waterlogged wood that I found promising.

When I suggested a walk, he endorsed the lower level of the new promenade, full of shadows and alcoves and the smell of the sea. Overhead, the tap and thump of footsteps, down below, the echo of the surf and the voices of other loiterers looking for excitement. A good idea. Even better was his notion to venture under the support pillars of the pier. We crossed the shingle beyond the lights and neon signs and slipped under the deep shadows of the ironwork. The incoming tide rattled the pebbles, a marine whisper running under the dance music, and he was very strong, very aggressive, very much to my taste altogether.

Intense moments, before a sudden surge of salt water surprised us as I was straightening my clothes and picking bits of rust out of my hands. I hopped to save my shoes, and we were retreating up the beach when a figure burst from the brilliant lights of the pier entrance and cleared the railing to slip and slide across the shingle. A woman, hampered by a sling on one arm, was running toward us, and I recognized her silhouette against the lights. "Poppy!"

With an anxious glance behind her, she stumbled over.

"Oh, Francis!" she said and put her hand on my arm. "Whatever are you doing here?"

"Looking for you."

Ernie laughed. "Who is this?" he asked.

"My cousin," I said. "Why were you running, Poppy?"

"It was the same man. The same man as in London." She shivered with distress. "I'm sure of it. He broke my arm," she told Ernie, who gallantly took out his fish knife and said, "We'll sort him for you," as if enthusiastic about trouble. There really is no accounting for tastes. "Just one of them?"

"I think so. I hope so."

Ernie looked up and down the dark beach, then took a glance at Poppy's shoes, not high but with a fashionable heel. "No point taking chances. If you don't mind taking off your shoes."

Poppy put a hand on my shoulder and slipped off her heels. I did the same with my shoes. Ernie led us back under the pier where the incoming tide crept almost thigh high. This is exactly why I dislike the seaside: stones underfoot, cold breezes above, and icy water in between. We had reached the other side of the pier supports when Ernie held up his hand. Someone was standing on the sand, watching the front I guessed.

"That him?" Ernie asked.

"Looks like it," said Poppy, who was wringing the water from her skirt. "He saw me at the phone box near my hotel, so he'll have a good idea where I'm staying."

"There'll be more than one probably."

"How do you figure that?" I asked.

"He's only watching one way, isn't he?"

Ernie had a grasp of tactics.

"Probably armed, too. One is fine, two with the injured lady here—not so good."

He correctly saw I would not be the best combatant. "Avoid the hotel," I told Poppy.

She nodded but looked miserable. "I don't think there's a train until morning."

"Seven a.m.," said Ernie. "You need a place until then, right?"

"Yes. Preferably away from here before we're swept out to sea." Nan's best encouragement had gone for naught; I can't swim.

"Plenty room yet." Ernie led us up the slope until the girders that floored the pavilions were only a few inches above our heads. We could hear the thump of feet on the boards above, and once in a while, a discarded cigarette flared down like a miniature comet. Poppy was shivering in her light dress and a cardigan. I gave her my jacket and shivered in turn. Ernie, used to gales at sea, sat stoically in his shirtsleeves and a vest. Periodically, he ducked around the piers to check the beach and the entrance to the pier where he'd spotted another loiterer. After a long and frigid time, he announced the all clear and led us back to the sidewalk, where despite her injured arm, my agile cousin scrambled over the railing and onto the pavement.

Approaching the midnight hour, there were still revelers on the pier and strollers catching a last breath of sea air but not enough of a crowd for complete safety. Worse, we must have looked a sight, our clothes wet with salt water well above our knees. We put our shoes back on and Poppy scanned the pedestrians anxiously. With everything looking normal on the seafront, a heavy mist in the air, and the promise of rain, not to mention our sodden clothes, I think she was tempted by her hotel.

"Not a good idea," I said, and Ernie concurred. "These were city folk after you, right?"

"I'd guess. I first spotted the man in London." She moved her injured arm. "Left me gun-shy."

"I know a place, not comfortable, I warn you, but nowhere a Londoner would ever think to look."

That sounded good to me, and Poppy was game as usual. He took us up the backstreets then turned eastward. When we returned to the shore, we saw the black silhouettes of boats pulled up on the shingle and a collection of disproportionately tall wooden buildings, set close together so that their roofs looked like the sharp teeth of a giant mouth.

"This is where we dry our nets," Ernie said. "Can't count on many sunny days here."

He opened a door and we stepped into weird shadows and the smell of salt and fish and other mysterious hints of the marine. "I'll be back before dawn. Keep quiet as you can and be ready to leave as soon as I knock."

With that, he closed the door and left us in pitch-darkness.

"Safest to sit down on the floor, I think."

"Another frock ruined," said Poppy. "Ouch. Oh, there's a sort of bench." She held out her hand for me and, after banging my shins, I sat down on a wooden plank beside her.

"Your pirate or whatever he is won't return to cut our throats?"

"He's a sailor. Part of the local fishing fleet."

"You really are a fast worker, Francis. How long have you been here?"

"Lizzie and I arrived this morning. We really did come to find you."

"I should have gone to London," she said in a reflective tone. "I should never have agreed to hide in a convalescent home, of all places. It's exactly the kind of Gothic pile mad wives were stashed in. I locked my door every night and tried to be on the Downs all day, but when I recognized the car, I knew I had to get out."

"The car?"

"The red-and-black saloon that Freddie used to borrow. It belongs to George."

"Lizzie's brother?" That was either implausible or alarming. "We drove his car here today, Lizzie and I. We parked in the main lot and walked half the town. She didn't stay over because she'd promised to have it back in good time tonight."

"Francis, I'm talking three days ago! I certainly would have recognized you and Lizzie."

"You're sure that it was George's car and that he was driving?"

"I was in such a state I *thought* it was Freddie. All this hiding in the woodwork is absolutely too, too bad. Of course, it was George! I recognized the license plate. I'd ridden in the car a number of times. Driven it, too, but naturally George didn't know about that."

I had the feeling, as Uncle Lastings would say, that we were about to go down the rabbit hole. "I don't think Lizzie knew he'd been here. If she did, she didn't mention it."

"I expect she didn't know," Poppy said. "Something for his work, I'd imagine. George isn't important. But seeing him reminded me of Freddie. It gave me such a shock, and I thought I had to leave. Confirmed by tonight's events."

I thought that George's visit was almost certainly important, but before I could explain anything, she continued in a rush. "Tonight I ate in my hotel—death by boredom and boiled veggies—and when it got late, I started feeling down and guilty and thought about calling Mother. I was in the kiosk and ready to dial when I saw the man in the brown suit.

"The same man with something about his walk. The kiosk light was on, so he had to see me, and I didn't want to be trapped in the box. I sprinted into a crowd and onto the pier. I thought I'd lost him. I was set to go back to my hotel when I almost walked smack into him in the crush. Luckily, he was looking in the opposite direction. I hopped the rail and ran down the beach. Where you called to me." She reached out and pressed my hand. "A sight for sore eyes, Francis."

CHAPTER 10

Poppy and I sat shivering together and talked through the night. Or most of it. I didn't hear Ernie's footsteps approaching, and I only surfaced from oblivion at a knock on the door. Thin bands of light were sliding through cracks in the siding, and a gray morning crept over the sill. "Ernie?"

It opened. "Better be on your way," he said.

Poppy stood up, smoothed her dress, stiff like my trousers with dried salt, and checked the daylight. "How far to the station?"

"Couple miles, but you can get a lift on one of the goods trucks. The drivers'll stop for a pretty girl any day."

We thanked Ernie and shook hands before he headed off to his ship with a wave. "You picked a very decent pirate," Poppy said. "You must have a better eye than I have."

She sounded so down, so unlike herself, that I said, "A lot of people were fooled by Freddie."

"That's just it. I've been thinking over what you told me last night."

I can see why Catholics pick little closets for confession.

Darkness, silence, and isolation are great encouragements to candor, and we'd had a general exchange of confidences. I'd told her about the autopsy findings and my lunch with Signor Rinaldi and the damage to the design studio.

"Oh, I'm so sorry, Francis! Poor Nan! I've gotten you into a pile of trouble."

I had to agree. When she got angry about the photo negatives, I reminded her that she'd left me to do my best. "Not good enough, Francis," she said and added other angry things, too, so that I curled up on the floor and did my best to go to sleep. But as we walked along the shore road, hoping for a lift, she returned to the topic. Though quick to anger, Poppy is basically fair-minded. "I was furious at first that you'd kept those negatives instead of turning them over to the police," she said. "Now I'm not sure I would have, either. It's terrible to lose trust in old friends."

I was interested to know just which friends had become unreliable, but a truck was approaching. Poppy ran a hand through her hair, stepped to the curb, and stuck out her thumb.

"Nicely done," I said as the brakes went on.

"Mother's right, always look like a lady."

I must have looked dodgy, for while there was room in front for Poppy, yours truly rode in the back with a cargo of turnips and onions. Poppy returned my jacket, so I was only semifrozen when we reached the station. I helped the driver unload his vegetables while Poppy checked the train times and bought all three of us cups of tea and bacon sandwiches.

Once on the London train, we had decisions to make. "What do you think I should do?" Poppy asked.

"Call your mother and go home?"

She sighed. "I feel so guilty about worrying her, but if I call, I'll surely be dealing with the police again. You think they believe me innocent, but they could easily have lied to you. And if you are right about Inspector Davis—"

"I don't know that I am."

"I think you might be. I've been wondering about the major's behavior. He and Eveline could have put off the Tollmans and the Groves if he'd been worried. Or he could have said that they had a party coming and there was no room for us to stay. Instead, he had Jenkins drive me to that isolated convalescent home. Besides, either he or Eveline lied about who found the blouse."

"A plant if there ever was one."

"Exactly. But stupid. That's what I can't figure out. Major Larkin was a military intelligence officer, a professional. Did you know that?"

"Lizzie mentioned that your father was in military intelligence. I guessed that might have been his connection with Major Larkin."

"That's right, and the major is, how did he put it, '*still semiactive*,' whatever that means. Surely if he was trying to implicate me, he could have come up with something more convincing." She was silent for a few minutes. "So I don't know what to think, and I'm not sure about going home. Or to my flat."

"Definitely not to the flat. I told you the building was being watched."

"Lizzie lives at home, but George has rooms." She bit her lip. "A week ago, I'd just have called Lizzie and made plans to stay for a few days with George."

I didn't need to tell her that was no longer a good idea.

"Lizzie was my best school friend." Her voice was sad.

"She did want to find you. She really was anxious when you didn't call again."

"I'm sure she was, Francis, but for what reason? She and George are very close. That's one thing. And the other is his visit to Hastings. A work meeting? Possibly. But at a seaside resort? Even a day ago I'd have said an innocent visit, now I doubt him and the whole house party—except for you, Francis."

I took her hand for a minute. "What do you know about George's work?"

"Electrical engineering. I know that's his profession. I don't really know what that entails . . ."

"Are you sure, Poppy? Lizzie said you'd become alarmed about Freddie's activities."

"Wasn't taking dirty pictures and selling them alarming?"

"You were surprised when I told you about that after his death. Something else must have led you to speak to Major Larkin."

Poppy looked out the window. After a bit she said, "You know I'm thoroughly ignorant, Francis. Sometimes people mistake that for stupidity."

"Was Freddie one of them?"

"I'm afraid so. George, too. They were good pals. I didn't think anything of that because George and Lizzie and I had run around together for years. Then Freddie appeared and fitted right in. So fun."

She didn't speak again for several minutes, putting her thoughts in order or deciding what to tell me. "I'm not supposed to discuss any of this," she said finally. "The major made that quite clear."

I bet he did. "I already know the half of it . . ."

"Right. And the major failed to make good arrangements."

Momentarily, Poppy sounded so much like her mother that I wondered if I was destined to turn into my father at some future moment. Life is full of frightening possibilities.

"He involved his friend Inspector Davis, who has connections with counterintelligence," Poppy continued. "I think that was even before Freddie's death. In fact, I know it was, because the major said more than once that his contacts wanted to know this or that. He was always hoping I would turn up something useful."

"Any specific area?"

She shook her head. "They had their eyes on Freddie, but they didn't really know which way to look, I don't think. All I could tell them was that Freddie had been after George for information. He asked so casually that I didn't catch on at first. He just had lots of supposedly friendly questions, *How's the project going? Still deep in invisible rays?* That sort of thing, but he was being a little too persistent, and I realized that George was unhappy and tense around Freddie—no more good old school friends. Though I was angry when you disapproved of Freddie, I began to notice that."

"Was he looking for information—or could he have been warning George, given that you were present?"

"I'm not sure I follow."

"By publicly mentioning George's work, was Freddie maybe hinting at some leverage?"

"Possibly. You're right that I didn't know then about Freddie's blackmail attempts. But I noticed some other things."

"Including Signor Rinaldi?"

"He was around, yes. He called Freddie's flat a couple of times, and if I answered, he pretended he'd called the wrong number. I recognized his accent just the same. So that was one thing. I mean, you can admire Mussolini, can't you, without getting involved with sneaky Italian diplomats?"

"I can't admire anyone with that much braid on his uniform."

Poppy slapped my knee and laughed before turning serious again. "Freddie had mysterious meetings, too, and I heard him arguing with George one day. I listened outside the door—you can see by that how uneasy I'd become."

"You're more the summon-the-troops-and-mount-the-charge type," I agreed.

Poppy nodded. "I could tell that he was threatening George, and I almost decided to have it out with him. But when I came in, he said, *George is really too selfish about that damn car.*"

"You accepted that?"

"I wanted to. I was really quite, quite besotted. More fool me. And maybe him, too. He might be alive yet if I'd spoken up."

"He was in a high-risk business."

She nodded unhappily without responding.

"And Rinaldi?"

"You were wrong about him. Well, I lied to you, so you would have been. When I caught them in the garden, I'm sure that sex wasn't on their minds. At least, not at that moment. They were having a heated argument, and Freddie was saying that he wanted money, a lot of money."

"Rinaldi offered me a hundred pounds."

"I'm sure that Freddie would have asked for more, much more. I distinctly heard him say . . . *absolutely vital for the air forces*, and he claimed he had a contact *at the design level*."

I'd guessed right—with a little help from Nan. "Ever hear of something called a cavity magnetron? Or microwaves?" I asked.

She shook her head. "Never heard of either, but George was not forthcoming about his work. Do you think that microwaves were the 'invisible rays' Freddie was asking about?"

"I'm guessing it's what he was selling, but I need to have the negatives printed. I don't like the idea of a commercial shop, though. I think we'd be better to find someone at least semiofficial."

"Not the major! We can't ask him, not if we're not sure."

"Inspector Davis is doubtful, too."

"Even if you didn't think he or one of his people tipped off Rinaldi, he's too close to Major Larkin," Poppy agreed.

We sat, listening to the monotony of the wheels, before I mentioned Nan's idea about Uncle Lastings.

"Uncle Lastings!" she exclaimed with an expression of distaste. Perhaps I shouldn't have told Poppy anything about our adventures in Berlin.

"He will know how to deal with the photos," I said.

"Well, from what you've said, he is a man for all weather. He is your side of the family, of course."

Poppy again sounded disagreeably like her mother. "It may

take time to locate him and to get everything organized. In the meantime, you'll need a place to stay outside of your usual set. I may know the right people, but the operative word is *may*; I'll have to talk to them."

"Do I sense complications?"

She didn't know the half of it, and I was determined to keep things that way. "When we get into London, let your mother know that you're not lying dead in Sussex. I'll call my friends and see about getting you situated, and then, yes, I think I must contact our uncle." Emphasis, you'll note, on *our*. She wasn't going to lop Uncle Lastings from her family tree quite so easily.

"And clothes, Francis. I smell like a salted fish and I could kill for a warm coat and a change of clothing."

An unfortunate turn of phrase. I must remind her to drop the homicidal exaggerations. "Nan might manage that. She claims no one notices an old lady."

"Ask her, please, to get some of my clothes from Mother. If she does that, I won't have to call." Seeing my face, she added, "Not cowardice, not entirely; it's in case anyone is listening."

Was that likely? I wondered. Could someone official or unofficial be even now thrilling to Aunt Theresa's critique of the latest butcher's meat or her struggles with members of the bridge circle? It seemed implausible, as implausible as the fact my frivolous cousin had thought of it, and yet— "All right, but all that will have to wait until we can get back to the studio."

We arrived, bedraggled, cold, and tired, at Victoria. Poppy was nervous and so was I, although logic said the police could not watch every single train from Sussex. In the event, we left the carriage with the commuter traffic and exited the station unnoticed by officialdom. When Poppy saw a small dress shop nearby, she insisted on buying a new blouse and skirt and a cheap cloche while I stood about courting rheumatics in my still damp trousers.

"You look like a shopgirl," I said when she emerged, newly kitted out.

She glanced at her reflection in a display window and pulled the hat farther down over her brow. "Perfect, don't you think? As long as I keep my mouth shut, who would recognize me?"

Who indeed, and we agreed that it would be safe for her to go to the studio. Avant Design was shut up tight with a new lock, but Nan was in residence. After she fussed over us for a few minutes, she ran through the various arrangements, concluding with the news that Mr. Mendelssohn could do the chair repairs anytime.

I decided to take them right away. Poppy wanted Nan to fetch her clothes, but I didn't trust Aunt Theresa's discretion. I argued for waiting until Poppy was safe elsewhere, and we went back and forth on this until Nan's offer of hot water for a bath settled the issue. I fetched a cab, loaded my damaged chairs, and set out for Mendelssohn's place in Hackney, a three-story build-ing with flats above an old-fashioned storefront with handsome iron columns. I noticed that the big plateglass window had a crack through one corner and that a piece of plywood was affixed above the door. Not good signs. I set off a bell as I entered and hauled the chairs into a narrow room with a counter, a cash register, a calendar, a map of London, and a doorway to what looked to be a substantial workshop.

Muriel answered the bell. "Francis!" I got a kiss. "And here's the damage!" She turned each chair and inspected it as carefully as if she'd been in furniture manufacturing half her life instead of cavorting in heels, sequins, and feathers. "Leather's a total loss. We'll scrap it up for eyeglass cases, that sort of thing. Oh, yes, nothing's too small. Waste not. But the frames look all right, nothing more than a few scratches. We know Sokolof; he does careful work with good material. You were lucky there, Francis."

She assured me that Ben would see the chairs were mended and produced their leather samples for my selection. I'd just made my choice when her husband appeared from the back, a long black work apron over his dress shirt and tie. He seemed pleased to see me, though I thought that he looked both thinner and more anxious. He checked the chairs and shook his head. "Terrible," he said.

"Small potatoes compared to Germany," I said.

"But how it starts, Francis. How it starts."

"Yes. We need to talk," I said. "I need a favor that you might consider. In return, I might be able to help with your situation, though honestly it would be a very long shot."

Ben looked at me for a moment and shrugged. "What do we have except long shots? But we must have tea first. That is the English way, yes?"

I said that would be lovely. Muriel plugged in the kettle and Ben brought some chairs so that we could sit down. We spoke of nothing of substance until Muriel had filled our cups and handed out biscuits. I'd been mulling over how best to proceed, but when the time came, I took the straightforward route.

"You read about Freddie Bosworth's death, so you'll know he was engaged. To my favorite cousin."

They looked shocked.

"Yes. A foolish move on her part. But here's the thing . . ." I outlined the events that had led to her exile at the seashore with a broken arm, scratched-up legs, and the threat of a prosecution for murder. "Though I think that's unlikely, I am sure you can see the danger to her even so."

"You believe that Bosworth hid something in her possessions?" Muriel sounded doubtful.

"I know he did, because I found it." I explained that Freddie had branched out from sexual blackmail to what I guessed were stolen scientific documents.

Ben looked puzzled and Muriel added something in rapid German.

"Ah, for the Nazis?" Ben asked.

"I think rather for the Italians. His contact from the Italian embassy, a Signor Rinaldi, drugged me at lunch, and I assume it was his paid thugs who stole my keys in order to trash my studio and frighten Nan."

"They are all fascists," Ben said.

"Right you are. A couple things are odd, though. Freddie was killed before he handed over the information." I described his abrupt departure and added that everyone, except Poppy and me, had an alibi of sorts, mostly from one another or from members of the domestic staff.

"Very convenient," said Muriel.

"Almost too convenient. For example, Tollman and Grove were apparently playing billiards all afternoon with Signor Rinaldi."

"Grove," exclaimed Ben in agitation. "Basil Grove, the furniture distributor?"

"I believe that's what he does."

"He knew Freddie Bosworth well! They were, what is the phrase?"

"Hand in glove," said Muriel. "As I told you before, when Bosworth was killed, we thought our troubles would be over. But he was just the public face."

"Grove has the cash," Ben said. "He funds the Blackshirts and anti-immigrant sentiment."

"That means Jews, here," Muriel said drily.

"So many of our people are small businessmen or artisans in furniture, fur, and woodworking," Ben added. "Grove gets support by claiming to protect British jobs."

"What he's really protecting," Muriel added, "is his own profit."

Her husband nodded. "He wants no competition. None at all."

"And Freddie? What exactly did he do?"

"We think that he was the bagman," said Muriel. "He went around doling out funds to the marchers and street fighters."

"And vandals," added Ben. "You saw our windows?"

I had.

"Third time. But it takes more than that to frighten someone from Berlin."

Although I could believe that, I knew that he must be worried.

"Grove is a rich man with contacts in government, with people like Tollman and Major Larkin," I said. "Freddie probably met the Italian through him."

"Who is this Tollman?" Muriel asked.

"Peter Tollman is something in finance, formerly a government functionary. All the Larkins' weekend guests and the lady of the house are big Mosley fans and New Party supporters."

"A nice group you've gotten into, Francis!"

"You can say that again, but blame a call for help from my cousin. Now she needs to lie low until I can get Freddie's information to an official without fascist sympathies."

"There are some fascists in your government," Ben said heavily.

"Too right. The excuse is that Mussolini is making the trains run on time."

"And you want us to hide your cousin," Muriel said. She didn't sound enthusiastic.

"I know it's a risk."

"Ben is in danger of deportation, thanks to the Blackshirts and men like Grove and your country house pals. Hiding a murder suspect would be the last straw. You don't know what you're asking, Francis."

"I have some idea," I said, "but she wouldn't have to be in your home. We just need an unlikely place for an ex-deb with right-wing connections. Think about it: Grove and Rinaldi have influence, and Freddie did, too. You need someone with good government contacts on your side. If what Freddie was selling is valuable, and I believe it is, we have a bargaining chip. To counter men like Grove."

"An ingenious idea but too much of a risk!" Muriel expanded on this so vigorously that I began to wonder if she and Poppy together might be a combustible mixture.

Ben waited until she paused for breath then said, "I disagree, my dear," in a quiet voice that told me he had thought things over carefully. "Yes, it is a big risk, a big danger. But we are already on the knife edge. Refugees—you may not know this, Francis—must be self-supporting or supported by the Jewish community here. They are not to work, so as not to take English jobs, but they are not to be a burden to the state, either. You see, even running a furniture factory and helping my distressed countrymen is a risky business."

Muriel got up and collected the cups and rattled the saucers and cutlery in an angry way. When Ben said something to her in German, she turned and shook her head.

"*Nein, nein!*" She took the tray into the back. When she returned, she said, "I have another idea. If your cousin is as game as you are."

"Oh, more so! Poppy is quite fearless."

"Well then, we'll hide her in plain sight. I still have contacts at the music halls and clubs. From the news photos, your cousin's a pretty girl."

"A stunner, according to those who know."

"Possibly athletic?"

"Very. Though not tall. Not nearly as tall as you."

"She couldn't get work as a dancer, not without training, except in a dance hall, and that's riskier in a number of ways. If she'd pass as a hopeful just up to London, I can probably get her taken on by wardrobe. I know where there's a temporary opening for a dresser. What do you think?"

"I think my aunt would die of shock, but it's brilliant. And it keeps Ben out of the picture. Lodgings, though? She must have a place to stay. And she can pay. She went off with some cash."

"Let me arrange that," said Muriel. "I know just about every cheap lodging for stage gypsies and dancers in London."

CHAPTER 11

Muriel was as good as her word. Within twenty-four hours, Poppy, still dressed like a shopgirl and mourning her fine wardrobe, arrived at the Royal Adelphi, where she was to help one of the headliners with her satins and spangles. My cousin would share a room in Soho with a dancer in the same cast, and she was supposedly a stagestruck country mouse. "You're shy," Muriel empathized, almost as soon as they met. "Say as little as possible, otherwise your speech gives you away."

Poppy nodded. I hoped that Lizzie was right about her theatrical talent.

Muriel explained the duties of a dresser. "The wardrobe mistress will keep you straight. Just pay attention to her. Basically, it's next costume always ready, mend everything that needs mending right away, store the costumes clean in the order they'll be used. Mostly common sense. And remember, the artiste always looks wonderful, whatever the situation. When you are doing several turns of an evening, your morale needs a boost."

"Luv, you look a treat," Poppy said.

I had to admit it was a fair imitation.

Muriel acknowledged this with a little grimace. "Don't overdo."

"Just teach me the right things to say, and I'll be fine." Poppy is nothing if not confident.

"Later," Muriel said. "Right now we need to meet Violet."

"I've seen her perform, you know." Poppy spoke with real enthusiasm. "She's wonderful."

"She's a trouper," Muriel said. "Swears like one, too. You'll get a taste. Don't take it personally."

I thanked Muriel and hugged Poppy before they went around to the stage door and disappeared into the theater. I set my own course for Soho, hoping to turn up my uncle. The difficulty was where to begin. Though his ideal lady, wealthy but tolerant, had so far proved elusive, he was still avid in her pursuit. To impress some rich widow, he might venture dinner at Kettner's or Chez Taglioni. With the boy of the moment—and there was almost always a boy of the moment—I could expect a far different venue. He'd select somewhere cheap and louche, saving money for little presents and excursions.

Venue was only one problem. As I knew from experience, even recognizing Uncle Lastings was another, because he was a real chameleon in dress and even hair color. That night I was lucky. I was passing a club noisy with American jazz when I heard, "Nephew!"

I turned around. There he was, splashed pink and green from the neon signs and togged out like someone in the City with a proper suit, a silk tie, and a bowler hat that covered his particolored hair, still growing out from the dye job he'd acquired as a Frenchman.

"Uncle Lastings! The very man I'm looking for."

He put a flirtatious hand on my shoulder. "The night is young," he said, but his look was ambiguous. Was he out for pleasure—or business?

"The evening must be promising when you are looking so spiffy."

"Isola Bella suit you? Very quiet and private there."

Isola Bella was a fine restaurant, almost in rich-widow territory. Though I was strongly tempted, I feared the walls might have ears. "I don't feel like Italian," I said.

"Well!" my uncle exclaimed. He gave me a shrewd look but, without further comment, led the way to a pretty French restaurant with decent pictures on the walls and big prices on the menu. My uncle was clearly known to the staff, suggesting he'd enjoyed a run of prosperity, and we were seated, as requested, in a small private room upstairs. Doubtless a favorite place for illicit deals of every kind.

"They do very nice fish here," my uncle said, "though *la belle cuisine* brings back painful memories of our recent rupture." He patted my hand. My uncle is never more dangerous than when he is pretending to be avuncular and sentimental. In France, even though he'd entangled me in a scheme that just missed disaster, he'd been displeased when I emerged with a profit. So I wasn't going to pretend to be his affectionate nephew, even if, in the amber light of a luxurious restaurant, he was still attractive.

He raised his eyebrows but said nothing more until our orders were taken. "So much to catch up on," he said. "I have followed your own career lately in the press."

"One pays for family loyalty."

Another quizzical look.

"You don't think I'd venture to a country house party for fun! You cannot imagine what a bore Major Larkin was about his architecture. The rest had only three topics: gossip, politics, and horses, and little new to say on any one of them."

"I was forgetting your tastes are strictly urban. Was it my niece, Penelope, who involved you?"

He had a serious interest if he was referring to Poppy as his niece. "I responded to a cry for help."

"Very gallant of you, I'm sure. But she's still missing?" His voice was casual but his expression showed his interest.

"Far as I know." I changed the subject, feeling it was too soon to trust my uncle with anything more. "And you. You're looking prosperous. Fit for the City and the bastions of finance? Or just a lady with more money than sense?"

"Bitter, nephew. Very bitter. Quite undeserved, too. Clothes make the man, and these make a serious man, consulted by those in the know."

"I hope so," I said. "Are they official and right-minded?"

"I did not know you had politics of any kind, Francis."

"I've seen enough to know what I don't want: men in ridiculous uniforms fighting in the streets."

"A description covering a multitude of sinners at the moment."

"I'm thinking Italian sinners, in particular. Any interest there?"

"Alberto Rinaldi, for instance?"

"The prime example. He invited me to lunch at Taverna Firenze."

"I've eaten at Taverna Firenze. The food is marvelous."

"But stay away from the grappa." I described the aftermath of our meeting, including the theft of my keys and the break-in at my studio.

Uncle Lastings shook his head when I finished. "Mussolini has agents all over London and sympathizers throughout the catering trades. Every other waiter is suspect, and even antifascist Italians can be pressured through relatives back home. In the circumstances, you were lucky to escape so lightly."

Lightly was a matter of opinion, but I agreed I was lucky. "They damaged my samples and destroyed half my designs, but the worst was they left Nan tied up and helpless. Who would have heard her if I hadn't come back?"

He shook his head in a show of sympathy. "Not to be thought of." He took another drink of wine before he asked, "But you and Nan are innocent parties? Signor Rinaldi and his cohorts were mistaken? You wish a word passed to that effect?" My uncle narrowed his eyes and assumed a grave expression. He really did look like a man with influence, though in what quarters was the question. Could he convince the government types I was hoping to influence? That was the question.

Nothing ventured, nothing gained, as Nan says. I took a breath. "On the contrary, I found what Freddie Bosworth was hoping to sell, and Nan hid it."

"Ah!" He raised his glass. "As I told your father years ago, you are a boy in a million."

"My father didn't need to be told that. He knew it and hated it."

"He is not a man of broad sympathies," Uncle Lastings agreed. "But I am impressed. And with Nan, too. Such a mind. A pity she is not younger and rich. I'd be tempted to set my cap for her."

It did not seem the moment to remark what a disastrous combination my rogue of an uncle and my dear nan would be.

"But what is this mysterious item?"

I described what I had seen in the negatives. My uncle was not terribly interested in Freddie's sex photos, commenting that they were probably now of "low value," nor did *cavity magnetron* produce a rise, but when I thought to add the mysterious name *Chain Home*, he sat straight up and his face grew not just serious but concentrated in a way I recognized. Although I find something comic about my uncle's elaborate schemes and disguises, I must admit he can bear down on a problem. Once he focuses his energies, his solutions are often both daring and effective.

"You are lucky to be sitting here," my uncle said. "And what was that other thing you mentioned?"

"*Cavity magnetron*? I looked it up at the BM. It produces electromagnetic waves, invisible rays that can find objects in the dark. Like ships in fog—or planes at night."

The penny dropped. "If that has anything to do with Chain Home, those negatives must be printed immediately. The project was just a name until now, but seeing at night!" He tapped his finger on the table. "The military implications are almost unimaginable! Time is of the essence, Francis. We'll fetch them as soon as we finish eating."

I put down my fork and wiped my mouth. "You're forgetting something. The negatives aren't a donation."

My uncle turned all bluff and military as if he'd just stepped out of his old regimental quarters. "Those documents may be essential to the defense of the realm. In the wrong hands, they could compromise our security, especially RAF effectiveness."

"At the moment, they are in the right hands. No one supports the RAF, England, and the empire more staunchly than Nan."

My uncle was not amused. He went so far as to threaten me before I was able to make it clear that money was not my object. Then I felt he was a trifle disappointed. He had been angry when I charged him to store his dodgy pictures; now he seemed sorry that I was not genuinely mercenary. The males of my family are a difficult lot, but eventually I got him to listen. "I could have been killed in Berlin," I concluded. "Sure, I had official help, but without Muriel, I couldn't have contacted the embassy safely. Now, although she's English born and bred, she could wind up stateless along with her husband, who's not only a good man, but too wealthy to be a drain on the exchequer. He should be an asset to England."

"But a Jew, Francis. And a German one at that. I needn't tell you they are not popular."

I shrugged. "Since when have you worried about popularity? You can be sure that document is safe with me, but without the other negatives, you may never know how Freddie got it. And the photos will be in the fire tonight without an agreement. Don't doubt I'll do it," I said and set my face. I've learned a few things from knocking about in shady places with the rough trade

I enjoy. Most important, how not to show fear. I am often frightened, not being superbrave, and, indeed, fear is as good as oysters in some ways. But showing fear is another matter; it brings out the worst and causes events to get out of hand. So I've learned to look calm and determined and indifferent.

"It will take time."

I shook my head. "Won't do. The powers that be need to make this quick. Tell them the offer is for a limited time only. Poppy has been hurt. Nan's been endangered. I've already been offered a hundred pounds, and I suspect I could get a whole lot more. A couple good passports is surely not too much to ask."

We went back and forth on this until, exasperated, I said, "Miss Fallowfield wouldn't hesitate. Neither would Mac." They had helped me out in Berlin, and I had done well for them.

My uncle sputtered about this for a minute, as if he found it hard to leave military mode. But eventually, he called the waiter over and paid the bill. We took a cab to Waterloo Station. When we were deposited outside the terminus, however, my uncle walked away from the doors toward a nearby tower block with shops and a petrol station on the ground floor. There was a guard inside the main door, and the whole place had a strong feel of covert officialdom, as if this was metaphorically His Majesty's little back closet or garden shed.

My uncle had an identity document. I had none, but I was vouched for in glowing terms. Finally, we were allowed to take the elevator to the fifth floor, where my uncle had access to an office with a telegrapher. "We will send in code to Miss Fallowfield," he said. "If she will vouch for you, the deal will go through."

He got a piece of paper and we constructed a message, basically exchanging potentially valuable material touching on Chain Home and security failures for bona fide UK passports and residence status for Muriel and Benjamin Mendelssohn, Hackney, London. My uncle handed this to the telegrapher.

"When can we expect an answer?" I asked.

"Before morning, I should think. Certainly tomorrow."

Uncle Lastings wanted me to fetch the documents immediately, but I was unwilling to do so without an answer. I commandeered a beat-up couch and settled down to wait. Berlin was an hour ahead, but it was still early for a night owl like Miss Fallowfield, who would be sitting up reading in bed if she was alone or at her kitchen table with cigarettes and whiskey if she was consulting with Mac. He'd be the one, I guessed, to bring her the message. They would talk things over and decide who they should contact, because an incident in London involving an Italian attaché was not really in her brief.

I had a vivid image of her long, thin face, and of Mac, ruddy and stocky, sitting across from her in the low amber-tinged light and even imagined the sounds of their voices, voices of old colleagues with complicated memories. I was acquiring a few of those myself, and they were beginning to blend in an odd way when my uncle touched my shoulder. I sat up with a start. I'd been far away, asleep, in fact.

Uncle Lastings nodded.

"I want to see the reply." I have learned the hard way that the best way to trust Uncle Lastings is to see the evidence.

There was a dispute about that, naturally, with the telegrapher burbling on about security procedures that seemed to me surprisingly lax. Finally, he sent another message, and we had another wait, and then there came a salty reply direct to me to the effect that the deal was on. I was shown this message, and when I saw the language, I had no doubts.

Uncle Lastings disappeared into the depths of the building to conjure not just a car but a driver. "Security, my boy," he announced and fairly bounced into the backseat. At Avant Design, we roused Nan from the alcove where she set up her bed at night. While I made her some tea, she got her sewing kit with her little razor knife and slit the wallpaper. "I think I have just enough left to mend this again," she said. After a bit of fiddling, she produced the two sets of negatives, each wrapped in a scrap of silk.

My uncle pocketed them eagerly. "You have the thanks of the nation," he announced grandly, causing Nan to raise her eyebrows and declare he'd best see that her dear boy was protected. Uncle Lastings reassured her so floridly that I understood he'd badly needed some coup to justify his expenses and favors. Now with the negatives in hand, he was entering his flamboyant mode, and part of his plan was to leave his nephew behind. I wasn't having that.

The content of the scientific document was undoubtedly beyond me, but Freddie's other photos were another matter. "I can help with identifications, particularly if anyone from the Larkins' house party was involved." I also emphasized Poppy's welfare. "She's in hiding and doesn't know who she can trust, not even among her oldest friends."

My uncle twisted his mouth as if he, personally, did not expect to trust anyone, old friends included, but he finally conceded that I might be useful. I said good night to Nan and returned with my uncle to the tower block just beyond Waterloo.

Another consultation with the lethargic (and clearly forgetful) security guard. My uncle repeated his earlier performance and we were permitted to enter the elevator. Up first, to collect a weary-looking gent with all-night stubble and dark circles under his eyes, identified only as Morris, then down below ground level to photographic services. The technician signed in the material, countersigned by my uncle and the night watchman of the security services, and we waited again. There was a pot of tea of mysterious origin and faintly chemical aftertaste. Also stale biscuits. I think such offices must buy them up when they are past their prime.

Eventually, the technician emerged with prints of the document. Morris took a look and livened up considerably.

"Important?" Uncle Lastings asked.

"Vital. It stays in our hands," he said and touched my uncle's shoulder reassuringly.

"Ah," said my uncle with satisfaction, and I thought that His Majesty's security services should be prepared for bills and demands.

The other photos were promised soon. Morris took the document upstairs, leaving my uncle and me to wait for Freddie's naughty bits to be printed. Fairly soon, we had a contact sheet and then prints. Several of the images were blurry, but as Uncle Lastings said, nothing a clever tabloid graphics

department couldn't have improved. Others were quite sharp.
I tapped one of a blond man up to something complicated
with a chap in a mask.

"You know him?"

I shook my head. "Not really. But there's something familiar."
It was late, I was tired, and various bits of my mental apparatus were operating in slow motion. But blond, broad face, even
features—I remembered studying Poppy's friend across the table
at Lyons. Shorten her hair, lengthen her chin, and Lizzie Armitage would have passed for a handsome boy. "If Lizzie Armitage's
brother resembles her," I said, "this could be him. George is in
electrical engineering and, according to his sister, involved with
everything innovative. Plus, he made a workday trip to Hastings
while Poppy was hiding there."

"She would recognize him?"

"Oh, undoubtedly."

"We will have this edited and you can ask her." My uncle tapped
on the door of the dark room and gave the order without asking me
if I wanted this disagreeable task. "Anyone else?" he asked.

I studied one of the blurred photos. "I couldn't swear to it,
but I'm guessing this is Peter Tollman. He's rich and well connected—and an alibi for both Basil Grove, the furniture magnate, and Rinaldi. I'm betting that Freddie was passing at least
some of his 'donations' to Mosley's outfit."

CHAPTER 12

'Ve found it a good plan never to trust my uncle. This is not to say that he lacks family feeling or other more interesting emotions. But as a general rule, suspicion is the best strategy. When he produced a carefully cropped enlargement—*Nothing to cause a maiden's blush,* as he put it—of the man who might be George, I pocketed it and promised to ask Poppy.

"Promptly," Uncle Lastings said.

"Too late tonight. Way too late." It was, in fact, well into morning

"I'll see you get a ride home, and I'll collect you in the morning." Clearly, my uncle had moved up in the shadow world. Was he hoping to advance still further with the discovery of Poppy's hiding place? I thought so.

"I can manage. I'll find a cab at Waterloo."

My uncle insisted on giving me the fare just the same, and I agreed to be ready at 10 a.m. Good luck with that! I caught a few hours of sleep at home, but as soon as Nan got up, I clued her in and skedaddled to Maurice's studio. He was snoring in the back, not being an early riser. That suited me fine. I lay down on the studio couch, wrapped myself in the assorted drapes he used as props, and managed another few hours of sleep.

It was close to noon when I woke up to a shout of, "My Pommy bloke!"

With one thing and another, I'd been neglecting Maurice, but soon, all was forgiven. We had a late breakfast with the big omelets he cooks so well and amused ourselves in the studio for a while afterward. Then I laid in the background of a fresh canvas for him with a deep ochre tint that proved troublesome to keep smooth and even. After that, we had glasses of wine and some slices of hard sausage and cheese. Thus fortified, I said I had to run an errand.

"Just when we were hitting our stride," Maurice said and pulled a sad face. "What can possibly take you away?"

"Favor for a friend," I said. "I'm hours late as it is."

Maurice is insatiably curious about my life. He pouted and teased so that I resorted to the movie dialogue we both love. "I'm off for king and country," I said, which had the merit of being true.

"Oh, do tell!"

"Top secret, old boy. My lips are sealed." I'll spare you the rest, except to note that Maurice sometimes fancies himself the male Mata Hari or, maybe, the lady herself. This time our frolics on the studio couch turned out to be ill-advised, because the playful spy got into my pants pocket and found the photo. Trouble!

Maurice quite enjoys scenes. He jumped up immediately, demanding to know who the handsome blond was, and I could see that he was prepared to be jealous and theatrical like a right old queen.

I'd had enough playacting for one day. I let him run on for a few minutes, then I said, "If you recognize him, please tell me. It will save me a difficult job."

He blustered for a moment more, but he'd detected the change in tone and sat down beside me, quite serious. "You really don't know him? Handsome as he is?"

I shook my head. "I'm off to see someone who might identify him. If you don't recognize him, Maurice, forget you ever saw this. Safest, really."

"You weren't kidding earlier?"

"Not entirely. My cousin is still missing. This man may be connected."

Maurice has a fine visual memory. He took the photo again and looked at it carefully. "I believe I've seen him." He shook his head. "Don't know his name, not a painter. Not a model, either." Another pause. Concentrated thought suits Maurice. I began to think he'd make an interesting portrait. "Chelsea Arts Ball! Last year. I'm sure of it. He had a gladiator helmet and a tutu. Mixed messages, I thought," Maurice added archly. "I do prefer a man who can make up his mind."

"Anyone know his name?"

"Now you want all my little secrets."

"Just this one." Now it was my turn to tease and coax. I finally got the names of a couple of Dilly Boys who might be useful.

"Davie and Wilbur. They were with him. Delphine and Wilma, they were that night. Oh, painted to the nines. And scented like a flower shop. You should have seen them." Maurice waved his arms and did a campy little turn.

I figured I'd have to search the town before I turned up either Davie or Wilbur, boys who might—or might not—be as gossipy and prying as Maurice. Still, they were a possibility if Poppy failed to recognize the photograph. I thanked Maurice, cautioned him again to forget the photo, and left the studio by the back entrance. Although I didn't think Uncle Lastings knew about Maurice, I wasn't taking any chances.

Such caution was possibly merited. As I approached the local Tube station, I had the bad feeling that I was being watched, even though I didn't see anyone suspicious behind me, and there was no one loitering when I stopped before a haberdashery window. Still, Poppy's stalker must have invaded my imagination, because I could not shake an uneasiness that increased when a man in a long dark coat followed me into the station. He wore a trilby pulled down low on his brow, and he stopped and fussed with a cigarette until my direction was clear. Then he followed a dozen paces behind me.

Although I told myself this was nonsense, I abruptly turned for the westbound trains, instead of taking my usual eastbound route. My shadow in the long coat made a similar decision. When the train came, he chose the same carriage I did, then stared indifferently out the window. Studying the darkness of the tunnel? Or watching me in the mirrored surface? Fortunately, the District Line was busy at that hour, and two stops along, I slid out just as the doors were closing and got into the crush transferring to the Piccadilly Line.

There I caught an eastbound train to Leicester Square, exiting to Soho, where I found Poppy's new address. It was a smoke-darkened three-story Georgian building that hadn't been fashionable since the Regency. There were three apartments per floor, and the stairs carried a lingering smell of boiled vegetables, fried sausages, and elderly drains; in short, the same corner of Bohemia that I'd inhabited on the Continent.

I knocked at the door of 37. The statuesque girl who answered had her hair in curlers and a cigarette perched in the corner of her bright painted mouth. She was wearing nothing but a silk teddy under her fluttering pink wrapper. When she saw me, she pulled the wrapper closed, crossed her arms, and demanded to know my business.

"Is Poppy, Penelope, in?"

She turned her head and shouted, causing the cigarette to flap. "You know a pudding-faced chap in a leather jacket?"

"It's Francis," I said.

"Says his name's Francis."

I heard my cousin's voice from the back, and her roommate stepped aside, giving me a glimpse of a long, muscular leg and a bare foot with the calloused toes of a professional dancer.

"Francis! I thought we weren't supposed to meet. We're just in a rush to get to work." Poppy's shopgirl's outfit was beginning to look a bit worn and she herself looked tired and a trifle anxious. Clearly, a busy life in the deb set was less exhausting than spending long nights at the theater as a dresser.

"This will be quick. A place to talk?"

"I'm doing my face," the roommate announced and disappeared into the back.

"That's Harmony, one of the lead dancers," Poppy said. "Brusque but a brick."

I sensed that she wasn't eager to learn the purpose of my visit, but there was no point in postponing the inevitable. "The negatives were developed. Would you look at this?" I took out the cropped photo. Her face changed as soon as she saw it. "You recognize him. Who is it, Poppy?"

"You're wrong. I don't know him, never saw him." She put her chin in the air defiantly, but I wasn't convinced. I could see that she was hurt.

"It's George, isn't it? Lizzie's brother."

"You're not listening, Francis! I just said I don't know him."

"You're not that good a liar, Poppy. I can find out from you or there are other chaps I can ask. But that will mean complications. Understand?"

Poppy bit her lip. "He's in trouble, isn't he?"

"I'm afraid so. But there's no proof of anything except that Freddie had the means to blackmail him. George might have given information to Freddie—or he might not have. We don't know. Either way, there are going to be questions for him."

Poppy seemed on the verge of tears. "Can't you just tear it up? Can't you, Francis?" She turned away momentarily and shook her head. "No, of course not. I know you can't. It's too late. But I wish to God you'd destroyed those negatives. Every single one. Please leave, Francis. Now! Or you'll be noticed for certain," she added and practically pushed me out the door.

Back down the stairs with those associations of Berlin and Paris. Did I feel a touch of the old familiar Continental paranoia?

I certainly did! When I spotted a phone box at the corner, I walked straight by, although I should have called immediately to confirm George's identity. But the side street was almost empty at that time of day. I felt conspicuous on the pavement, and the idea of being enclosed in a windowed phone box unappealing.

Instead, I headed over to Berwick Street, where the market would still be busy, and I would be just another stroller amid the sidewalk stalls, the late shoppers, and the various touts and schleppers drumming up customers with their aggressive patter. *There's safety in numbers, Francis!* I was walking quickly, head down, and thinking about my cousin and her nice friend, Lizzie, and her blackmail-prone brother, when two men appeared out of the shadows. My heart jumped, as if my body recognized them before my mind. They moved to either side of me and pushed me into a dark and narrow lane with a row of dustbins and broken window sashes and mysterious heaps of waste and rubbish.

I dug in my heels. I had no intention of venturing farther into that sinister area. Immediately came the click of a flick knife and a glimmer off the narrow blade that came to rest against the side of my throat. I had a sudden image of Freddie lying bloodied in the grass.

"You've got something we want," one said. He had a heavy Italian accent.

"I doubt that very much. I don't have as much as a pound on me." I added, "*Non ho soldi,*" for good measure.

The one with the knife stepped so as to block the view of any curious passerby; the other slid his hand into my pockets, exclaiming triumphantly when he produced the photo. I should have destroyed it before I left Poppy! But no one pays up for a head shot, even if the expression is suggestive. The older one realized that. He was heavy with a Garibaldi beard to compensate for his shining bald dome, and he clicked his knife shut and shook his head in disgust. The other, who was much more in the style of the neighborhood with a flashy striped suit, brilliantined hair, and pencil mustache, burst into excited Italian. When his colleague refused to share his enthusiasm, he grabbed the front of my jacket and rocked back on his heels as if to head butt me.

I wasn't having that. I brought my knee up into his crotch. He released me with a gasp. I stumbled back against one of the heavy dustbins, caught the handle, and tipped it against his bald colleague who, momentarily off balance, swung his knife at me. I felt a cold sting along my neck and made a lunge for the head of the lane.

With a gulp of air and a desperate burst of speed, I skidded onto Berwick Street and into the big open market, where I plunged into the narrow passage between the stalls and shop fronts, bumping proprietors and dodging the schleppers who called their wares and badgered passersby. The awnings were down against a fine drizzle and their shadows and the bare electric lights in the shadows gave the market an exotic air. I slipped behind curtains of "silk" stockings and squeezed past store windows holding lingerie—a personal temptation—while corset sellers, stout and armored like dreadnoughts in their products, held their ground and provided interference.

Farther on were produce sellers and fishmongers and men and women selling sausages and tripe and liver and bread, all eager to see me and prepared to barter, but shouts from behind told me that the two Italians were still in pursuit. I was trying to spot them when I almost ran into a tailor's boy struggling to push a rack of finished suits with one hand and hauling another behind him that held pinned and basted garments—a near impossible task in the crowd.

I moved next to him, half crouching and hidden by the suits. "I'll give you a sixpence if you let me push one rack," I said with a glance behind him.

He was small and dark, with a thin face and the stooped shoulders that come from piecework and long hours with the needle or the sewing machine, but quick. He followed my glance. "Fascistas?"

"Yes," I said.

"I'll see your money just the same."

I put one hand on the forward rack, and as we shuffled through the crowd, the boy occasionally shouting for room in both English and Yiddish, I fished up a sixpence and put it in his hand.

"Them's finished garments! Both hands on the rack!" With this command, we picked up the pace. The crowd parted for our combined approach, and we managed to reach Oxford Street, where the fancy shops and fancier shoppers provided extra protection. Nonetheless, I stayed with him until we rolled the racks into the goods entrance of a big shop. Immediately, he started swearing in all his languages: He'd noticed blood on my neck, and when I put my hand up, it came back smeared red.

I stepped away from the clothes rack, and the boy frantically checked every inch of the jackets and trousers. Fortunately, the damage was confined to my own shirt and jacket, and after the store receiver, official in a white shirt and a long pin-striped apron, had entered the goods on his sheet, the boy calmed down. By that time, I was sitting on the floor with my handkerchief pressed to my neck, wheezing as I always do after running and feeling more than a little weak and woozy.

Once the all-important garments were stowed, the receiver, small and dark like the tailor's boy but with a plump face and a complaisant expression, approached with a semiclean towel. Now that all was well in men's suiting, I was a matter of interest. My neck was wiped; the towel turned red. The resourceful shopman fetched his teakettle and poured a good deal of water over the wound.

Then he and the boy held a consultation. A long but shallow cut was their diagnosis. Despite their business in fabrics, they did not seem to have any scrap linen for a bandage. Their solution employed the tools of their trade. The boy whipped a thin curved needle from his lapel and the receiver scrounged a hank of silk thread. The boy threaded it with practiced ease and after another wipe of the towel, squeezed the edges of the slash together and slid the needle painfully into my skin.

What he lacked in gentleness, he made up for in speed, and soon he whipped off a knot and cut the thread with his teeth. The receiver leaned over to inspect his work. "Very neat! A surgeon couldn't have done better! You are so lucky. Such hands Jakob has!"

I thanked them both and tipped my surgeon another sixpence. The receiver then put on the kettle, being of Nan's persuasion that strong tea with sugar is, like whiskey, a genuine cure-all. We drank our tea and denounced the fascists, and after the tailor's boy left and I'd had enough blood removed to look presentable, the receiver led me through the back corridors to the main shop floor, where I feigned interest in a number of frilly trifles until I was sure the coast was clear. I hustled to the nearest Tube station and made my way home. At the corner of our street, I stopped at the phone box. I dialed the number my uncle had given me, and as soon as he picked up, I said, "It was George Armitage."

CHAPTER 13

You might expect since I had secured the negatives in the first place, conveyed them safely to the authorities in the second place, and identified a suspect in the third place, that I would be in my uncle's good graces. That I would be, as he was wont to say on special occasions, "one in a million." You'd expect nothing less, but I am sorry to say you'd be wrong.

The next morning, having gotten a proper bandage around my neck and a good deal of coddling from Nan, I was enjoying a late breakfast when Uncle Lastings thumped at the studio door. Nan had just left to do the marketing, and I wouldn't have put it past him to have waited until he saw her go out. Wise of him if he did, for Nan was down on officialdom that morning and blaming my uncle for my *slashed throat*—an exaggeration. I had a big oozing scratch, now stained sienna with Nan's iodine, but otherwise, no lasting consequences. Just the same, a little sympathy from my uncle and sincere congratulations would not have come amiss.

Instead, what did I get? Not only my uncle in a foul mood

over his spoiled plans and ready to fault me for the decline of the empire, but also my least favorite copper, Inspector Davis of the chilly eyes and mysterious agendas. The two of them were united in displeasure, because George Armitage had left both his work and his flat and disappeared.

"I can't think why you're surprised," I said, although I was both surprised and alarmed. With so much else to worry about, I'd found it easy to assume that George was wedded to his invisible waves and mysterious generators. "He must have suspected that his name would come up. Why else was he in Hastings that day? He either thought Poppy knew something or hoped Freddie had left her the documents. So he was already suspicious then."

Such an appeal to reason did not impress my uncle. "Had you met me yesterday morning at ten as we'd agreed, we'd have had the identification within the hour, and George Armitage would have been picked up before lunchtime!"

"You didn't need to know where Poppy was. Nobody's been concerned about her safety."

"That young woman tipped off the suspect," said Inspector Davis.

"You can't know that," I said, although as soon as he mentioned it, I thought it likely. The urge to phone George, or more likely Lizzie, would explain Poppy's haste to get me out of the flat. "He'd have been at work. I doubt she knew his number."

"But his sister would have known and she and your cousin are good friends. He left his place of work roughly two hours before you called Lastings. Because you delayed that call, Armitage was warned and had time to slip away."

"I was prevented," I said, touching the bandage on my throat. I had downplayed the incident with Nan; I gave my uncle and the inspector a much more dramatic account.

But Inspector Davis proved as heartless as my uncle and equally unreasonable. He was *unalterably opposed to civilians in any investigation*, but when I heartily agreed, he pulled a sour face and said the least I could do was to *help retrieve the situation*.

I didn't like the sound of that at all. I liked the plan they'd concocted even less. Basically, I was to be the goat while they played Great White Hunter. I flatly refused.

"Too bad about your friends," the inspector said.

I looked at him.

"The Mendelssohns."

"Davis here is Special Branch. Were he to suggest that the Mendelssohns are a security risk, your deal would be off," Uncle Lastings said and added, "Don't think even Clarice Fallowfield could buck that," in a tone that told me how much he'd disliked the arrangement.

"And here I'd assumed I was immune to blackmail," I said, but they were too shameless to take offense. One really is in Oscar Wilde territory when one's virtues are more dangerous than one's vices! We went back and forth for a while, but it was clear that in protecting Poppy, I'd put Muriel and her husband in real danger. "All right," I said finally, "but I must leave a note for Nan."

They didn't like this, either, and started on about security and discretion.

"If Nan comes back and I've disappeared, she'll call the

police, the papers, and the lord mayor of London," I said and saw my uncle give Davis a slight nod. They looked over my shoulder as I wrote that Uncle Lastings and a colleague had asked for my assistance. *I'm not sure how long I'll be, but don't worry*, I concluded.

"Right," said Uncle Lastings. "Into the breach!"

Beware of my uncle's enthusiasm, especially when he adds military metaphors. "Exactly where are we going?"

Inspector Davis shook his head. I reluctantly locked the studio and followed them to a waiting car. My heart sank as we turned south into the green and pleasant countryside. Now that I was trapped, Inspector Davis unfolded the details. They were worse than I'd feared. Not only was I supposed to be peddling the very documents that were now safe in the hands of His Majesty's government, but I was to do this at a little party at Larkin Manor.

"Surely you're joking! Rinaldi has tried to get the material twice by force and once by purchase. Why now? It must be obvious to him that any meeting with me will be a trap."

"Rinaldi," Inspector Davis said with a sniff, "has diplomatic immunity. The most we could do would be to have him sent home, and that is not necessarily in our interest."

"The devil you know," suggested my helpful uncle.

"So Tollman and Grove," I said. "The sex photos, yes, I can see that. If we're right that's Tollman in one, he'd maybe pay for it. But Grove? What's his interest?"

"Same as Freddie's, we think," Davis said. "Leverage to get information."

"But George has disappeared."

"They don't know that yet, hence our haste."

"Too much for my taste. Grove and Tollman must still be suspicious."

"We're counting on them being nervous. The major has handled the matter very well. He's let them know that you'll be down for a little historical recreation." The inspector made it sound perverse and gave me a sly look. "Quite plausible, actually. He's started a dig just beyond the Norman tower and has unearthed postholes or pots or oyster shells. Great excitement, and you are thrilled beyond measure. Remember that."

It sounded worse than antique brasses and Jacobean furnishings.

"He let it slip at his club that you'd be coming down."

"Wait a minute," I said, "you were setting this up even before George Armitage did a runner."

"There is still the matter of Bosworth's murder," Inspector Davis said calmly. "Anyway, they were both charmed with you—or so they said." He looked dubious. "And they asked to be included in the party when you arrived."

"They are dropping everything midweek to be charmed by my company?"

"They are clearly after something," said my uncle. He put his hand in his pocket and pulled out two little packets. "Copies of all the negatives."

"Except for the document," Davis added. "We faked something up, because we can't risk the real thing."

"Hide these carefully. One or both may want to avoid paying."

I asked him what he thought they were worth. "Rinaldi wanted to give me a hundred pounds for everything."

"He'd have gotten promoted for sure with that deal," said Davis. "But a hundred pounds for the sex photos? A nice round number, I think."

"We don't know who else is in them, do we?"

"That's something we're hoping you can find out," said my uncle.

What a nice tête-à-tête that would be! But irrelevant. "George is the important one. If he's the one who got Freddie the material about Chain Home—"

"Don't even mention that name," Inspector Davis warned.

"My point is that George'll have the information right in his head."

"The precise reason we need to find him before the Italians or someone else does. If he agrees to work with a foreign power, we lose the advantage of the project. If he refuses, they'll kill him to be sure the project is delayed. They profit either way."

Poor Lizzie, I thought. "He's really that important?"

"The man's a bloody genius," said the inspector. "A bloody genius blackmail-courting poofter."

I shrugged. "He wouldn't have been blackmailed if His Majesty's government was more enlightened. We could have had more plays by Oscar Wilde, too."

Clearly Inspector Davis was not a theater fan. "There's danger and then there's danger," said the inspector. "He'll be lucky to escape alive."

"So why are we fooling about with a furniture magnate and a probably dodgy financier?"

"They are committed fascists," Uncle Lastings said. "We know they are in touch with the Italians. They may know where Armitage would hide. Or they might be acting as go-betweens."

The inspector nodded. "If Armitage tries to leave the country, we have a good chance of intercepting him. But if he's gone to ground here, Tollman and Grove may be our best hope."

Talk about the artistic imagination! Their whole plan rested on assumptions and hope. Worse, I suspected that they had other agendas yet to be revealed, and I was not in a happy mood when we pulled into the station one stop north of the manor's. "We can't drive you to the door," Inspector Davis said, "but don't try to leave the train or to continue on to the coast. If you are not at Larkin Manor within the hour, I'll see that both Mendelssohns are detained, preliminary to deportation. You can count on it."

My uncle gave me a return train ticket and handed me a valise. "What's in here?"

"Dinner clothes. And an informal kit for your work on the dig. I've assured Major Larkin that you can't wait to get your hands dirty."

We were standing behind the open trunk of the car. "Can I trust him?" I asked too quietly for Davis to hear.

For the first time, my uncle seemed uncertain. "I believe he's loyal," he said, "but safest to trust no one entirely."

I thought that must be my motto. A quarter of an hour later, I stepped off the train. Larkin Manor was a mile and a half away by road, less by the farm lanes. With no sign of a cab, I decided to defy fate and take Freddie's route to the manor. I climbed a bar way off the main road, skirted a harvested wheat field, and reached a network of footpaths and farm tracks. Within ten minutes, I spotted the rubble and ruin of the tower, and, behind it just visible through the trees, the complicated roofs of the manor itself. I must be in better shape than I'd imagined. Or, more plausibly, Freddie must have had more time around the manor than we'd figured.

I wondered how long he'd been lurking behind the house before he was killed. And how many people he'd managed to see, because I didn't really credit all those alibis. With good questions without obvious answers, I was almost glad to be distracted by the sound of metal hitting earth. The dig, no doubt. Perhaps my asthma would play up and I could be excused.

I rounded the brushy corner of the base of the tower. Between it and the stables was a quite level stretch of ground. *I learned to ride a pony there*, Poppy had said. Now it was set off by stakes and ropes. A burly fellow with a muscular backside was swinging a pickax under the major's direction, and when he turned at my greeting, I recognized the agreeable Jenkins. A possible glimmer of light in the rural darkness!

"Walked from the station, did you? You might have called for Thorne," the major said.

"It was no bother; I took a shortcut." In fact, the country air was already causing me to wheeze gently. I hoped the major would notice, but he immediately launched into the implications of his find. "A kitchen midden."

When I looked blank, he added, "We won't find the glamorous stuff. No, no. But the essentials of life in a remote stronghold. Meat and drink, wouldn't you think, for the National Trust?" I detected a faint note of desperation. Perhaps the National Trust had been less than enthusiastic about opening its purse. "There are fancier places, more distinguished architecture, I admit that," the major continued, "but here we have the whole history, even bones and pots and broken tools. Look at this." He held out a shard of pottery. "Recognize this?"

It was a lumpy grayish-green something. I turned it first one way and then the other. "Looks like a piece of an egg cup."

The major laughed. "Same shape, that's right, but it's a lamp. Eleventh century. Maybe even tenth. Jenkins here always goes for the earlier date."

Jenkins had stopped work to lean on his pickax, and he held out his hand for the lamp fragment. I was interested in how carefully he examined the piece. "All handmade," he said to me. "No potter's wheel back then."

"Amazingly primitive," agreed the major, and the two of them stood with their heads together studying the brittle remains of some long-ago housemaid's breakage. "I'm sure you can see the importance," he said to me finally. "But go change. I know you'll want to get some time in on the dig."

I paid my respects to the butler and to the housekeeper, who said that Lady Larkin was unavailable. In my room, I looked for a likely hiding place for the negatives, but every possibility seemed vulnerable even to a lazy chambermaid, never mind a dedicated searcher. Finally, I stuck them in the pockets of the caramel-colored corduroy pants my uncle had mysteriously chosen for the dig and went off for some historical recreation.

The major and Jenkins were deep in the newly excavated ditch. They had pinned a tape measure to the cut, and while Jenkins read off the depths of the different layers, the major wrote them down in a notebook. Presently, he sent me to the stable for a pail of water and, when I returned, set me to washing the finds of the day, the homeliest assortment of broken crockery imaginable.

We worked until the light started to go and Jenkins announced, with what seemed amazingly like regret, that he was needed for the dinner preparations. "The guests arrive on the 7:06," he reminded the major.

Major Larkin stuck a marker into the last recorded layer and told Jenkins to carry on. When he was halfway to the house, the major set his notebook alongside my collection of drying pottery and got down to business. "You've been briefed by Davis?"

"Up to a point. A good deal seems to be left to improvisation."

"The key thing," the major said, "is that all conversations of a personal nature should take place in the billiard room." He raised his eyebrows to see if I understood.

"Right." So Davis or my uncle or the major would be listening on some obscure connection. Cloak-and-dagger stuff but reassuring in a way.

"That's it then. See what you can elicit from Grove and Tollman."

"Do you think they killed Freddie?"

"If they did, they didn't gain much, did they?" He took out his pipe, fiddled with the tobacco for a moment, then lit it. "I suspect they wanted to, but they're amateurs."

He spoke in such a cool and reflective way that I wondered exactly what he was. A nice old architecture buff, the henpecked husband of a rich and politically ambitious wife? Or a cold

ex-intelligence officer with a loyal batman and the experience
to distinguish between amateur and professional homicide? I
decided that the sooner I could stop washing pots and unload
those duplicate negatives, the better.

But first dinner. Or, rather, first, a stroll about the manor to
find a place for the negatives. Perhaps, as Nan maintains, honest labor clears the mind, because as soon as I entered the main
hall, I spotted the major's pride and joy, that elegant and insa-
lubrious pioneer WC at Larkin Manor. Confident that no one
was around, I slipped inside. Attar of ancient drains. A big tiled
basin. Lovely decorative tiles on the walls. I hoped for a loose
one, but finally I climbed onto the fine mahogany seat of the toi-
let and tucked the little packet with the faux document negatives
behind the plate of the flushing mechanism. I decided to keep
Freddie's action shots in my pocket. I eased the door open and
returned unseen to my room to await the dinner gong.

The party turned out to be gents only. The formidable Lady
Larkin was shopping in London for her daughter, Victoria, who
was sampling the delights of Il Duce's Rome. Was that a spur-
of-the-moment trip if her wardrobe needed topping up so soon?
And if it was, had Victoria gone to breathe the air of the Modern
State or for other, more sinister, reasons? I began to understand
how suspicion and paranoia spread like ripples on a pond.

In any case, we were four at table, attended by Jenkins, who
was dressed, to my disappointment, in plain black instead of his
ornamental knee breeches. We had soup and fish, followed by
a roast, and lots of good port. Despite this lubricant, it was an
awkward, wary party. We were all eager to get down to business,

but no one wanted to broach the crucial topics. I think even that battle-ax Lady Larkin might have lightened the atmosphere.

Such general conversation as there was mostly concerned the excellent food, while the major filled in the longer silences with updates on his various architectural projects and on the dig. At various times, I was called upon to express admiration for the finds and delight at my participation. I managed with such a straight face that Nan would have been proud of me.

Mostly, though, I studied Grove and Tollman. On first acquaintance, they had struck me as being much of a muchness, although with probably fifteen or twenty years between them. Now I took a closer look and realized that Tollman was not as old as I had figured. Confidence had lent him maturity at our last meeting. Now, with strain and preoccupation making him look less impressive, I realized that his fetching silver hair was probably premature. He wore it so long that it flopped over his forehead, and he had a habit of running a hand through his locks and flipping them back from his brow. He was luxuriously attired, too, finance, inherited money, or government service had been good to him.

Grove, Muriel and Ben's enemy, was not as smart looking but more talkative. As the port bottles emptied, he gave us his wisdom on trade, immigrants, Mussolini, preparedness, and taxes before venturing into the airy realms of *what must be done.* Nothing he said was original, and I was beginning to doze with my eyes open when I caught an echo of Signor Rinaldi: "One supports Mussolini in order to awaken England. Il Duce's Italy provides the model for the Modern State, militarized by a strong leader with the capacity to enforce change."

He sounded like a propaganda pamphlet and I looked at him: bluff, red faced, well fed, serious, and absolutely, smugly confident about everything, including, if we were correct, selling national secrets. No wonder the Mendelssohns, already acquainted with a so-called Modern State, feared and disliked him.

Tollman, I have to say, did not look so certain about anything. He must have realized that he'd been compromised, and I guessed that saving his reputation had gone to the top of the list, ahead of leading England to greatness with a lot of black uniforms and gold braid. Had either he or Grove killed Freddie and then lied to protect his secrets? Maybe, but unless they turned on each other, such a case would be hard to prove, especially since Rinaldi would have his own reasons for keeping quiet.

Up at the head of the table, the major began a long and circuitous story that appeared to be about leadership in the trenches and concluded with the suggestion that we retire to the smoking room. "Or," he added, as if an afterthought, "the billiard room. I know you younger fellows like a game." Jenkins was commanded to bring brandy, and we retired to smoke and drink until the major decided, on the slimmest evidence, that I could play snooker and proposed a match between me and Tollman. "All right with you, Basil?" he asked Grove. "Too dark to look at the dig, but Francis here washed up a lot of the recent finds. Let me show you some little bits of ancestral history!"

He put his hand on Grove's shoulder and they went out. Tollman handed me a cue and racked the balls.

I put down my cue. "Let's get to business," I said. "You'd wanted to buy something from Freddie?"

Tollman looked acutely uncomfortable. "Freddie was black-mailing me."

"Freddie had bad habits."

"There's a certain picture. Wouldn't do for public consumption."

Nor for the home front, either, I thought and nodded.

"What do you want for it?"

"One hundred pounds."

"A hundred pounds!"

Interesting reaction. A hundred quid was a substantial sum, but he certainly looked flush. I shrugged. "I have another buyer. It's all the same to me." I really thought that he would break down and pull out the cash or make some arrangement, but he began to plead poverty.

"Besides," he said after a minute, "how can I be sure it's the only photo?"

"It's a negative. And I only found a couple."

Tollman was not reassured. He picked up a ball and began tossing it up and down nervously.

"Of course, we might do a swap," I said after a minute.

He stopped. "A swap?"

"What was Freddie after? Besides cash in hand."

"Information."

"Care to be more precise?"

He sniffed and ran a hand through his remarkable hair. "Freddie, you know, was something of a tactician. He had connections with a variety of people, and he was always trying to gain leverage with someone."

I waited.

"Lately, I got the impression that he was working for the Italians, that he had some big deal afoot with that slimy Rinaldi. I wish I had never met either one of them!"

I could believe that.

Tollman paced back and forth beside the billiard table before he said, "It was Grove who introduced me. Freddie was with Mosley's outfit then. Not the BUF, not the riffraff—the New Party people, some of them good men with good ideas. At the time, Freddie seemed like an all-right chap."

"With interesting friends?"

Tollman nodded miserably. I must confess I wasn't terribly happy with the situation, either, because for a minute, I understood him all too well. He hadn't left his version of Ireland; he hadn't had someone like Nan who loved him just as he was; he'd tried to fit in. That had worked for a while. Good job, nice clothes, fancy wife. And then he'd met Freddie's interesting friends and all the compromises came apart and he wound up caught on camera without his pants. Naturally, Freddie had started to blackmail him. For money first, I'd guess. And then with the current political situation, for influence, information, contacts. "You'd been something in the government, I believe."

"Nothing terribly important. Undersecretary-to-the-undersecretary type of post. But as an investor, I'd been watching the electrical industry, electronic equipment, coming things, you understand."

I did. "So you knew some interesting people, too?"

He nodded.

"I need a name," I said.

"George. George Armitage, genius engineer. I saw him at some parties. With Freddie. I was able to find out what he was working on."

"And you mentioned that to Freddie?"

"He already had his claws in George, but yes. I was able to confirm his importance. Nothing more."

"Do you know any of George's friends? Or any favorite places of his?"

He shook his head.

"What about Basil Grove? Did Grove know him, too?"

Tollman hesitated. "No, he didn't know him. But he knew about him, I think." He stopped and looked troubled. "I'd forgotten. Basil said something about Freddie's wanting a favor. I gather it involved meeting with George sometime that weekend."

"But you don't know what it was about?"

Tollman shook his head. "All moot, of course, after Freddie stormed out. He liked drama." "And he liked to involve people. He would have said that the Reds or some antifascist outfit was following him, but probably there was no more to it than that he wanted Basil to look complicit. That was very much his style."

"I tell you what," I said. "Give me fifty quid and we'll call it even."

Tollman argued this, but his protests were all for show. A few minutes later, he had the duplicate negative of himself in flagrante delicto and I had his pound notes. He almost immediately relaxed, the expression of strain vanished, and he was once again a member of the top nation and completely respectable. A man I now liked less.

"Lucky for you in a way," I remarked.

"Lucky? You've just picked my pocket for fifty quid."

"I meant Freddie getting himself killed. Though I guess you'd be a prime suspect without that alibi from Grove and Rinaldi."

He was confident enough now to laugh. "You see me as likely to push a man off a tower and cut his throat? Let me tell you something. I don't know about you, but everyone else that weekend had a motive to kill him." He saw my doubt and added, "Our hosts included. If you're going into Freddie's line of work, I suggest you remember that."

CHAPTER 14

Tollman didn't hang about. He freshened his brandy and disappeared, glass in hand. I wished for London or, failing that, for a rail connection offering immediate French leave. But no. Even if I slogged the mile or so to the station, there would be no service until morning. And if I did manage to catch the earliest morning train, I didn't doubt for a minute that Inspector Davis would set about making trouble for the Mendelssohns.

Even though he must have gotten an earful! My best hope was that he'd been listening in directly. My fear was that the major would instead retrieve a recording and find out that Tollman not only suspected his entire household but had passed his suspicions on to me. That would not be good.

My only inspiration was to empty the decanter before canvassing the room. I hardly knew what to look for— wires, I supposed, and some type of microphone and maybe a wireless-like box, a sort of receiver in reverse. I looked under the billiard table and behind the curtains and lifted one of the omnipresent canine portraits, for, as if real hounds weren't enough, the manor featured a kennel's worth of painted dogs. I was examining a massive radiator when someone coughed.

I was startled, I admit. I turned to see Grove standing in the doorway. "Basil!"

"Game over?" There was something distinctly unpleasant in his tone.

"Before it began. Peter's too skillful for me."

He moved to the table and began toying with the cue ball. "Surprising, that. Peter doesn't really think strategically."

I shrugged. "What about you, Basil? Do you think strategically?"

"I like to think so. I always take the long view." He leaned his elbows on the table, and I wondered if he was a bit drunk. That could be to my advantage.

"You knew Freddie," he said after a moment.

"Not well."

He nodded complacently. "A complicated character. I probably knew him as well as anyone, given that I saw to his political education."

That raised my eyebrows. As far as I could see, "political education" had simply enabled Freddie to expand his dodgy operation.

"You are skeptical," Grove remarked.

"I knew him just well enough to be skeptical."

"Nonetheless, he was killed for his beliefs. A martyr for the future."

That was one way of putting it. "I'd have said he was killed for his blackmail habit."

"The one supported the other," Grove admitted. "The revolution sometimes has to use unattractive tools."

"That certainly describes Freddie."

There was a pause, suggesting that Grove was ready to get down to business. "And you, Francis?" he asked finally. "Are you interested our country's future?"

"I could do with fewer twits and more intelligence," I said. "Or are you asking if I've taken over Freddie's line of goods? Minus his political airs and graces, naturally."

"Freddie," Grove said carefully, "sometimes acquired useful material."

"Useful here? Or elsewhere?"

"The New Order does not necessarily respect traditional borders."

That sounded ominous. "Freddie's stock in trade was compromising photos."

"Not my interest. I don't share the public school weakness for pretty boys or flogging—or is it flogging pretty boys?" His grating laugh suggested he was not as calm as he seemed.

"Well, then, I'm afraid we can't do business. Freddie's specialty—" I didn't get any further before Grove grabbed the front of my jacket. Though only a couple inches taller, he outweighed me by fifty pounds or more. I backed into the billiard table and groped for a cue, thinking to crack him in the throat.

"He had promised Rinaldi something, something he insisted was good, very valuable. Not dirty pictures, understand?"

"I do speak English. Let me go and tell me what you have in mind." To make the point, I slid the tip of the cue into his groin. He released me and stepped back a pace.

"He'd gotten onto some scientific thing," Grove said. "Formulas or a diagram or maybe some new electrical system."

"Sounds pretty vague. You're sure this was a useful item?"

"Freddie was convinced it was. He said he wouldn't let it go for less than five hundred quid."

"What's your best offer?"

"Then you have it?" he asked in an eager way that set off alarm bells.

"Freddie's compromising stash included negatives of a document. Couldn't make head nor tail of it, myself, but I've kept it safe. For a price," I added.

Grove smiled and reached into his pocket for a stubby pistol. "Here's my best offer. Give me the negatives and you go home intact."

At this point in the flicks that Maurice and I so enjoy, the proper line is "you will never get away with it." The fact this popped into my mind indicated I was in danger of losing focus. Blame that last brandy. I swallowed the cliché and instead asked Grove if he'd killed Freddie. In response, he swore and waved the gun around and threatened me with everything from a slander prosecution to a bullet. I hoped that the inspector and my uncle had dropped their headphones and were racing to my relief. With that in mind, delay seemed the strategy. "It will look bad," I said. "Shots fired and all that. Every visit a murder—that's not going to look good for you."

He leveled the pistol at me and pointed out that even a nonfatal bullet wound could be painful or permanently disabling.

"Just to be clear, Grove, you intend to give possible scientific or military secrets to the Italians." *Let them record that!*

"To the future," said Basil Grove, and his ringing tone made me think he might really believe all that rot about new politics making new men and a shiny new future. I thought I'd been dealing with a rich entrepreneur with an eye for the main chance. Someone I could understand. But if I was dealing with a fanatic, that changed the equation.

"How do you know they don't already have them? Rinaldi's been looking since the morning Freddie died. For all you know—"

He gestured with the pistol. "Enough," he said. "You're a rum character, Francis. Your death could wrap up the Bosworth case very nicely. I can tell you that no one's happy to have the investigation hanging on. You'd do for it and who would complain?"

Only Nan, I thought. *And maybe Poppy and Maurice.*

"The negatives," he said now and held out his hand.

"I don't have them on me, having foreseen—"

"Get them. And drop the cue."

Did I have an alternative? Could I see myself to some bit of Sexton Blake derring-do? I could not. "All right," I said. "Follow me." Down the hall, into the foyer with the major's historic WC, a *quiet and private place. Not the time, Francis, to remember snatches of poetry!* But relevant in this case, the *quiet and private place* being the grave. Wasn't that a little warning from the subconscious that the tiled WC was a trap? My heart jumped the way it had when Grove appeared at the door of the billiard room: *Think, Francis! Quick! My room? Servants' hall? The elegant stair where a foot might slip?* Suddenly, I had a better idea. "We have to go outside. I thought anywhere in the house too obvious."

"The place is a great bloody mausoleum," Grove complained.

"Well, I chose the dig. I was working there this afternoon, as you know."

He gestured toward the front door and I turned the latch, hoping for a clatter to alert the staff. But no, all was oiled and nearly soundless. *Let it be dark*, I thought, *pitch-dark*, and opened the door. Wind slapped our faces with rain. The manor grounds were robed in murk rather than the velvet blackness that would have been ideal. Grove was angry just the same. "We need a bloody torch," he said. "And it's wet. Everything will be ruined."

"They're wrapped in oilcloth," I said. "Freddie was a pro. And I wouldn't risk a light, if I were you. Too obvious at this hour." When he hesitated, I added, "I know the way. I was running between the damned dig and the stable pump half the afternoon."

Grove stuck the pistol in my back. "Hurry up then."

I took a breath. My eyes had adjusted enough for me to see the irregular outline of the tower and the long roofs of the barns and stables. Now I must concentrate. *Visualize the dig, Francis!* According to Maurice, the great Degas wanted pupils to study the model upstairs but paint or draw in a room below. So, it could be done, the maze of trenches being nowhere near as complex as a nude figure. Was that a stake? One of the major's markers? Yes, it was, and with that I had an image of the geometric patterns of grass, topsoil, and chalk, of stakes and sticks and occasional piles of debris: a green, buff, and brown Mondrian plus clutter. I had it in my mind's eye and I started forward briskly, causing Grove to protest.

"There's a risk in hanging about," I said, slowing only a little.

I skirted the big open rectangle where the major and Jenkins had found their pottery and headed onto a band of turf no wider than a sidewalk with exploratory trenches on either side. The grass was wet and the turned-up earth slick. What was in my mind? Nothing but delay and improvisation. "Corner here," I said and stepped onto another stretch of turf, yes, a little narrower yet. Wasn't this the one that Jenkins had warned me not to use, not even for a shortcut?

A cry behind me and I jerked away as Grove tried to seize my arm. Off balance and heavier than me, he broke loose a patch of turf and tumbled into the trench, discharging the pistol. I fell but managed to evade the drop, and I got back on my feet, slipping along the slick edges until I reached a wider path. Behind me, Grove shouted something and the pistol discharged twice more. I was certain he was right on my tail, and when I saw the stakes and ropes of the perimeter, I hurdled the last trench to land flat on the wet grass, slithered through some nettles, and dived for the nearest shadows, the shrubbery at the base of the tower.

Wet stone, weeds, brambles, a small tree that I grasped and swung around into the greater darkness of the tower. I should have explored it with Poppy; I should have a map in my mind. Instead, I was caught in the impenetrable darkness I had hoped for with Grove. A bang and ouch as I caught my shins and again as I fell forward onto my hands. A step. Steps. Of course, access to the levels of the tower. I didn't stop to consider whether I might be as easily trapped in a Norman ruin as in the major's antique water closet. Grove was down; I was going up.

The interior stair had pie-shaped treads, uneven and badly

worn with loose rock here and there. But it was dark. Let Grove
try his aim in here! Old dust was the downside, and the effort of
climbing strained my lungs. I pressed on, sometimes bent over,
feeling my way step by step up the corkscrew stairs until a gust of
rain hit me in the face. I had reached the top. A platform? There
must be some sort of floor. And hopefully a parapet? I'm not
terribly fond of heights, especially heights with no clear barrier
between solid stone and thin air.

Better find one, Francis! I froze for a moment and listened,
expecting to hear Grove's heavy tread, his impressive vocabulary,
the crack and ricochet of an experimental shot. Or worse. Grove
denied that he'd killed Freddie, but had he been up in the tower
with him? Would he know the stairs, the extent of safe foot-
ing? In some ways, silence was worse than the certainty of his
approach. I reached forward as far as I could and felt my way
along the stones. One foot, two feet. I took the last step and
lamented the abandonment of the snooker cue. With it, I could
have tapped my way to safety.

I edged a foot instead. I wanted to get away from the steps
and around the wall of the stairwell to what must be the level
area visible from the lawn. Once out from the shadows of the
wall, I should be able to distinguish the outlines of the building
and get a view of what was happening below. Desirable developments! Yes, indeed, and yet I stopped with one hand on the
broken interior wall, listening to the wind and rain and waiting for some sound from Grove, or better, a shout from Uncle
Lastings or the inspector or even the major, whose absence was
now suspect.

Nothing, nothing at all, but I had a sense of something amiss, some warning. From the lower depths of my subconscious, as Maurice would say? Or just the unpleasant memory of Freddie's body sprawled near the base of the tower? The latter was much the more likely, and I stepped around the interior wall onto the remains of an upper floor, heavy Norman construction with missing stones possible. *Go canny*, Nan said in my ear.

I could just make out the jagged outline of the exterior against the murk, and I was stepping toward it, checking the stone floor for gaps and holes, when I was struck a heavy blow from behind, knocking me against the not nearly high enough wall.

"Give them to me!" a voice cried. Not Grove. I was sure it was not Grove. Then who? The thought of some unquiet spirit flickered through my mind but disappeared at the shout—"Those negatives!"—as someone definitely of the here and now grabbed my arms and tried to wrestle me to the ground.

I began yelling. "I don't have them! Not with me! Let me go!" But nothing did the trick. My assailant stopped trying to knock me down and began punching me. I took advantage of this to swing around and attempt a few blows of my own, quite ineffective given the blinding wind-driven rain, the dark, the slick stones underfoot, and the height of my attacker. "Who are you?" I shouted. "What do you want?"

"The negatives. The document negatives!"

Before I could answer, I felt the terrible sensation of going from solid to not solid at all, to a stomach-dropping, total-body-seizing plunge. I felt the rough edge of the broken wall scrape my side and heard screams. Then nothing. A blank.

❖   ❖   ❖

Moments erased from time before I was aware of water on my
face, a pain in one thigh, something mysteriously wrong with my
left shoulder, and a lot of twigs and sticks. Also a light.

Grove had been wanting a light. Could that be him? What
the hell, I called out anyway, and the light swung around,
revealing my situation. No wonder I felt strange! I was lying
on a big shrub, make that halfway into a big shrub, several feet
above the ground, which was why, come to think of it, I was
shouting and feeling strange and in a fair bit of pain instead of
lying unconscious with bad things about my spine like the late
Freddie Bosworth.

I tried to extract myself and heard the major's voice: "Don't
move just yet."

He had a light and something else that glimmered. Without thinking—because I was clearly not in the self-preservation
mode—I said, "Please, don't kill me."

With a click, the blade of the flick knife disappeared. Just the
same—and without any real evidence—I guessed how Freddie had
died. Knowledge I'd better keep to myself because this was dangerous territory, up in the crumbling tower territory. Had the major
attacked me there? Unlikely, when he was standing quite intact
and mobile, instead of impaled on shrubbery or lying motionless
like the figure I could just see on the ground. "How is he?" I asked.

The major went over and had a look. Or maybe a second
look. "Out cold, but he'll live, I think."

"He wanted the negatives."

"Yes. It's George Armitage, I believe."

"He wasn't—" I said before I lost the train of thought in a hubbub of shouts and lights. Several men with flashlights and an improvised stretcher had arrived. They were moving about in a purposeful way, and I recognized Jenkins's voice. "Shift him carefully," he was saying. "In case it's his spine."

My spine was fine. All extremities moving. My problem was a burning sensation in my thigh that was becoming sharper by the second. The pain brought my mind back into focus, and when Uncle Lastings peered into my face, I said, "Armitage wasn't a traitor. Not entirely. He was trying to get the negatives back. About Chain Home. He wanted—"

"Enough of that," warned my uncle. He was joined by Inspector Davis, and more important, since he seemed to be the medical expert, Jenkins. The Agreeable One took in my situation and said, "Bloody hell! We need a hedge lopper."

That sounded so bad I did the sensible thing and passed out. When I came to, I was in the backseat of the Inspector's car with my naked left leg propped on rolled-up towels and what appeared to be a sprig of shrubbery protruding from my thigh. "I feel sick," I said.

"Oilcloth everywhere, lad," said my uncle. "You're on your way to hospital."

"And Armitage?"

"Ambulance for him. He has a brain worth millions, they say."

The sedan went over a bad bit in the road, and I passed out again. My last thought was that safe in his ambulance, George Armitage could take care of himself.

CHAPTER 15

I don't recommend the piercing of any body part whatsoever. You can put that in capital letters, even though the attending physician nattered on about my good luck that shrubbery had broken my fall. Otherwise, propelled beneath the weight of what he called "the other participant," I might well have been killed. I can tell you that before they gave me a shot of morphine, I was uncertain about the merits of survival.

However, a jab in the buttock, and I floated gently above the surgical table and the cares of this world. At some time in the night, the nursing sister topped up the shot, and I woke for good the next morning with my leg propped up, a drain in my thigh, and a six-inch length of twig left as a souvenir on the table beside my bed, right next to the metal pan for when I was feeling queasy. Nothing good there!

The first positive development was Nan's arrival. She came escorted by the surgeon who regaled us by describing how he'd extracted "half a foot worth of American elderberry" from my leg and a variety of "toothpick-size" fragments from my back. I was still too doped up to be appreciative, but Nan thanked him and shook his hand and set about examining my injuries for herself.

"Cuts and bruises mostly," said the surgeon. "His back should heal up nicely once he can get out of bed. The leg we'll have to watch, given that the branch was certainly not sterile." He pointed out the drain that he'd inserted, now carrying away a quantity of dubious red and yellow fluids. He added that even if I threw a fever, there was little cause for alarm, thanks to a recently introduced drug that was "very effective against infection."

Nan sniffed at this, being a great believer in iodine, the stronger and more liberally applied, the better. However, I saw her face change when she examined the twig and saw the massive bandage around my thigh.

"You watch him," the doctor said, "and alert the sister at any time if he seems feverish."

Feverish I wanted to avoid, preferring to remain what my old Latin teacher called compos mentis and chat with Nan. Uncle Lastings had fetched her, which was interesting in itself, and she had closed the studio and caught the first train south. "We must get you back to London," she said.

You can bet I agreed with that idea, and Nan said that I must have an ambulance to travel home and considered how best to convince the medical people. Then she read me a little P. G. Wodehouse that made me laugh until my leg hurt. I only agreed to rest when I began feeling distinctly woozy. I've discovered that morphine, which has delightful effects on the brain, comes with a wretched aftermath for the stomach.

"I'll get a coffee and come back," Nan promised as I closed my eyes.

The light was low when I woke up. I'd been in the tower, feeling my way across the ditches of the dig, and the major was on a sofa reading a novel. I knew it was the major although it didn't look like him at all, and the sofa, on reflection, looked a great deal more like a heap of Norman pottery or maybe an elephant. "Where am I?"

"Dear boy! It's all right." That was Nan. In the real world, not the dream one.

"Where am I, Nan?"

She said I was in the hospital in Hastings and pushed the call button. A sister arrived, starchy and official, to take my temperature.

Whatever it was, she declared that my leg needed examination, and she began the excitement of unraveling the bandage. Where it stuck to the wound, she snipped the fabric away with scissors and lifted the sticking bits with a pair of tweezers. I believe I was shouting at that point, and the sister called for reinforcements, including the surgeon who could identify shrubs from branches and who was up on all the latest drugs.

A consultation followed. I believe I was babbling, thanks to another shot of morphine. Floating above the bed on a cloud of opiates, I saw the doctor leave and return with what looked like a saltshaker. He proceeded to season my wound. His mouth was moving, talking to Nan. A sensible choice since I was far beyond conversation. The drain was checked and fresh bandages applied.

My newly acquired plumbing reminded me of the major's antique WC, currently hiding phony documents. I started to explain about this to Nan, then nothing.

Night. I woke up, more or less in my right mind, to a familiar clicking sound, the night sound of my childhood: Nan knitting through the long summer twilights or by the light of the oil lamp that warded off nursery terrors on dark winter nights. Knitting socks and sweaters for me and for my brothers and sisters, and, during the late war, socks, caps, and balaclavas for the troops. *Who are you knitting for?* I used to ask, and she would say, *For a soldier far away.* That night in the hospital, it took me some time to work out that I was not still dreaming, that Nan was actually in the room, her long needles moving at top speed.

"Knitting for a soldier far away?" I asked.

"One near to hand," she said, coming over to the bed. "Feeling any better, dear boy?"

"I think so, but I'd like some water."

Shortly, the sister arrived to take my temperature and bring a bedpan. The results passed muster: My fever was dropping and my kidneys were working.

"We'll let him sleep through the night," she told Nan and added that she should get some rest as well.

I felt wide awake and reasonably compos, but almost as soon as Nan resumed her knitting, I dropped off to the rhythmic clatter of the needles. I don't know how long I was asleep, but it was still deep in the night when I was jerked awake by angry shouts and a struggle around my bed. To explain those, I must rely on

Nan's account, and on the less coherent reports from the nursing
sisters and the doctor, and fill in the gaps with imagination.

So, envision the room: Dark it would have been, the shade of
the tall window drawn down against all but a sliver of the moon-
light, and the low corridor lighting reduced to a glimmer as the
door was mostly closed. Nan in the chair near the window, doz-
ing, I expect. Her knitting with the needles in the work resting
on her lap, the ball of wool dropped to one side. The bed curtain
on the window side was still drawn partway, and I was lying in
the darkness, the sides of my bed up in case my fever spiked
again and I attempted, as Nan said I'd done earlier, to leave bed,
room, and hospital on some fool's errand.

Then the near soundless opening of the door. Have I ever
mentioned that my nan has both the eyes and ears of a cat? Oh,
yes. No unauthorized exits from her nursery under any condi-
tion whatsoever! No unauthorized entrances, either. She opened
her eyes on a shadow. One of the nursing sisters? No, someone
wearing trousers and a surgical mask but with a white coat—*dear
boy, it practically glowed*—instead of surgical scrubs.

When she saw that he had something pointed—a needle? a
knife? a syringe?—in his hand, Nan shouted, "Stop!"

That's when I woke up, mouth dry, thigh throbbing, stomach twitching. A rattle as the bed rail on my left side was low-
ered. One hand pulled roughly at the bandages on my thigh;
the other held something shiny, something pointed, then Nan's
familiar voice was raised in anger. I saw the long gleam of a
knitting needle and heard a shout before the figure staggered
and fell against the bed, his arm grazing mine, the impact of his

weight on the mattress sending a jolt of pain through my thigh like a knife. I saw blackness and flashes, but he was the one who screamed, a dreadful sound, beyond pain into something else more terrible, before he reared up and whirled away, knocking Nan to the floor.

Running feet, shouts in the corridor, the door flung open. As the room lights came on, I grabbed the bars on the right side of the bed and hauled myself up. Nan was lying on the floor with a sister beside her. Another sister appeared at my bed. "Are you all right? Were you hurt?"

"What about Nan? Is Nan all right?"

"Yes, dear boy, no more than a few bruises." She sat up and got her feet under her. "That was no doctor."

"Certainly not!" The head of the ward was indignant. "No further medication had been authorized for this patient, not by anyone on the staff."

"He had something in his hand," Nan said. "An ice pick or maybe a syringe. Too large for a needle. He was trying to open Francis's bandages and get at the wound."

"He gave the most terrible scream," I said. "Perhaps when you hit him, he stuck himself."

"Whatever he had, he was up to no good. Dangerous no good," the sister said, and we all agreed, which was fortunate because one of Nan's long needles lay bloodstained on the tile floor. She hadn't hesitated, and I had a moment to imagine all that could have gone wrong before I reached out and pressed her hand.

"We'll get you back to London," she said. Music to my ears!

❖   ❖   ❖

She took that up with Inspector Carstairs, the local man, when he showed up bright and early the next morning, having dispatched his sergeant in the wee hours to sit in the hallway and keep watch on my room. He said that his hands were tied. "The matter is now up to Special Branch and the Yard."

She next tried Inspector Davis, who arrived shortly afterward. As I was no favorite with the London inspector, I figured he would be eager to have me gone, but I was wrong. I was apparently vital to the inquiry on a number of levels, and he wanted my account of the events at Larkin Manor. I did my best, although, without morphine, I had not only a throbbing leg, but a myriad of stinging and aching cuts and bruises. He already knew about my meeting with Basil Grove, who he said was lying a few rooms down in traction for a badly broken leg.

"Unfortunate," he added in a peevish tone. "Without that accident, we might have discovered his contacts."

"He had a pistol and threatened to shoot me. I wasn't so worried about his contacts as my survival."

The inspector made mollifying noises and asked me to continue. When I finished describing the events in the tower and my, admittedly vague, remembrances of the aftermath, I asked about George Armitage.

Inspector Davis sniffed in irritation. "Likely to live," he said. "Remembers nothing useful."

"He was certainly knocked unconscious," I said, but I thought that a little memory loss might be George's best chance to avoid the noose if not prison. "And his scientific abilities? Are they gone, too?"

"There's hope that his invaluable brain is otherwise intact. They're taking him to Cambridge to assess his scientific capabilities as soon as he can be cleared to travel." Both Inspector Davis's face and tone were sour.

I was not exactly well disposed toward George at that moment, but fair is fair—and Lizzie Armitage was a nice girl if maybe not totally reliable. "He wanted to get the document back. That's what he was yelling about when he grabbed me. Could he have attacked Freddie, too? Come in on that late morning train to confront him and followed him back as far as the tower?"

"And cut his throat when he didn't cooperate?"

I shook my head. "I doubt that. Not when he hadn't gotten the negatives and didn't know where they were. Besides, someone else must be involved, because that wasn't George in my room last night, was it?"

Inspector Davis shook his head. Before he could advance a better theory, Uncle Lastings arrived, full of praise for Nan, who he felt was wasted on yours truly. She had given him her account of events before resuming her efforts to get me back to London, and he wanted to compare my version to hers. Unlike the inspector, whose focus was on Tollman, Grove, and poor George, my uncle was interested in my attacker. Initially, I attributed this to family feeling for his nephew, but there I was wrong. After I had given the best description I could, he opened a little notebook and read me bits of her statement. "She claims the intruder was wearing a mask?"

"That's right. A surgical mask like for the operating room. And definitely male. He didn't speak, at all. Just that scream. Two screams. When Nan stuck him with the knitting needle and then a truly dreadful cry."

"This was when he was attempting to inject something?"

"He was trying to unwrap my bandages. And that was odd. If he had a hypodermic needle of some type, he could have stuck me anywhere and been successful, couldn't he? For some reason, he wanted at the wound. In trying to remove the bandage, he delayed just long enough for Nan to stab him with her knitting needle. He was thrown off balance and fell against the bed. I think the syringe or whatever it was must have stuck him somehow."

"But nothing touched you?" My uncle was very insistent on that point, and when I'd been as definite as I could be, he and the inspector examined the bed carefully and insisted that the sheets be changed immediately.

What seemed like an excess of caution made me nervous. "What do you think was his weapon?" I asked finally.

My uncle shook his head. "Time will tell," he said.

"In the meantime—"

"In the meantime, we wait. If your account of events is accurate and my supposition is correct, your attacker will not just be known soon; he'll be dead."

CHAPTER 16

Talk about Nemesis. There are times when the schoolboy's Greek and Latin stories come to life in alarming ways. But why wasn't I cheered by the prospect of quick retribution? Because until the attacker was caught—or, as my uncle predicted, turned up dead—I was to remain in the hospital. To my protests, and Nan's, both the inspector and my uncle had the same response: We were vital witnesses who could more easily be protected right where we were. Both of us were properly skeptical about that!

Besides, we were told, if I went up to London, there might be complications with the addition of what Inspector Davis called "new elements." I supposed these were Signor Rinaldi's cohorts or Grove's fascist colleagues, but I doubted that they would be any worse than our hospital attacker with his mysterious weapon.

I thought the sensible thing would be to announce that compromising documents had been recovered. As indeed they could be, given that some genuine negatives and a phony scientific paper were hiding behind the flushing mechanism in the major's historic WC. This idea was received with horror.

So instead of returning to pavement, soot, and civilization, we were stuck with the delights of the autumn seaside. Various constables and sergeants haunted the hospital, Nan was billeted at a nearby bed and breakfast, and the two of us were expected to languish in the odor of disinfectant and bedpans, waiting to see if Uncle Lastings was right that my night visitor was doomed. Day two of my stay was not too bad; I was still seriously under the weather. By day three, I was up and out of bed and thinking about the increasingly precarious finances of my studio with the many incomplete plans and drawings, and even more, about certain new images that seemed fit for canvas.

I began to complain to my uncle and to the inspector, and when I got no joy from them, I suggested to Nan that we might make our way home on our own. She plumped for an ambulance, but I strode around the room—well, strode is an exaggeration, but I stepped out in a convincing fashion—and said I could manage a taxi to the station and a seat in first class. I expected Nan to be enthusiastic, but she shook her head.

I insisted that I was on the mend, that I'd manage just fine.

"I believe you would, dear boy, but I would feel better if we knew who attacked you."

"Uncle Lastings assures me that he will be out of action."

"I never put too much stock in your uncle's assurances."

"There is that." I sat back down on the bed. "Not Grove or any of his British fascists, I don't think."

Nan shook her head. She had gotten cozy with the nursing sisters and seemed privy to hospital gossip. "The sisters say he is incommunicado. His leg is in traction, too."

"And George Armitage is under guard with a head injury."

"He was taken up to Cambridge this morning. The nurses were talking about it in the hallway. Some thought that they were moving him too early."

"So George is out. Tollman just wanted to get his photo and forget the whole business."

"Very sensible of him."

"And the Italians. They want the document. Killing me wouldn't get it for them."

"We've eliminated everyone," Nan said.

"Well, not quite. Tollman said something. In the billiard room." I stared into space and tried to bring up the room with its dark woodwork and the stained-glass lamp over the table. "He said that everyone at the house party had reason to want Freddie dead. I took that to include the Larkins."

"Ah," said Nan. "And the major was military."

"Military intelligence. Like Uncle Lastings and Inspector Davis."

"But he wasn't in any of Freddie's photos, was he?"

"Not that I saw. But who knows what Freddie knew. It might not have been about the major, either. Mrs. Larkin is very keen on the BUF and Mosley. She's the one who really knew Freddie."

"And the daughter, what's her name?"

"Victoria."

"Victoria went off suddenly to Rome, didn't she?"

"That's right. But there's something else. The night I fell. The major got there first. Alone. He had a knife in his hand, and I remember that I said something to him, that I said . . ." I was afraid the words were gone. The rattle of a cart in the corridor, the constable of the hour greeting one of the nurses, a gust of wind rattling the window, then I remembered. "I asked him to please not to kill me."

Nan took in a breath. "He would have thought of Freddie. He would have guessed you were suspicious."

"But I had no proof, Nan."

"He wasn't to know that. And if he had some strange military poison, he might have hoped to get away risk free. We need to talk to your uncle and Inspector Davis."

"I suspect it won't be news to them. They must know a great deal more about Major Larkin than we do."

"But they will not want to know," Nan said. "As officers and gentlemen, they will delay and delay if there is the slightest chance he is innocent."

"And he might be."

"We will call the inspector," Nan said, "and tell him that you tipped your hand. Understandably."

A walk down the hall, longer than I'd remembered, where I waited while Nan negotiated with the sister for the use of the phone. She was gone quite a long time, and when she returned, she looked discouraged. "Not available. But I got an Inspector Carstairs."

"He's the local man in charge of the original investigation."

"He's coming to see you," Nan said. "I sense he's been rather cut out of the investigation."

"Another reason to think the major might be implicated, though he has supposedly been assisting the Special Branch."

Carstairs arrived as I was getting my dressing changed. He

looked as doleful as a bloodhound and, as usual, reeked of tobacco. A few minutes' conversation proved that Nan was correct: He'd been told nothing and he was resentful. I soon saw that my nan planned to take advantage of this. She told him that *her dear boy* needed to get to London, and she wondered if he could arrange a car. She did not need to mention that that was the price of our information.

Carstairs considered a moment then nodded. Nan smiled, and I began recounting the events, omitting only references to the famous document, original or phony.

"Two of the people involved are in already custody," he observed. "One, of course, has been removed from my jurisdiction."

"He is supposedly invaluable elsewhere," I said.

"But the major. What reason could he have?"

"Larkin Manor. He's been living beyond his means to hold on to it, and he is desperate for the National Trust to take over the estate. Either Freddie knew something to block that or he was the reason the major was always short of cash."

"Possible," said Carstairs. "And you appeared to have taken over Freddie's business."

"That's right. That was the impression I was told to give. But since Major Larkin had set up the house party, I assumed that he had been filled in about my exact role."

"Not if he was a suspect from the start," Carstairs said sagely. "We have wheels within wheels here."

I agreed with that.

"You were lucky. He might have cut your throat."

"Apparently, he—or whoever attacked me—had a better

weapon. Something that would not be detected. Something secret, possibly military."

"Very likely military." Carstairs spoke with unusual animation. "Hence the complete shutdown of information. We've had a shocking lack of cooperation."

"We've been told that if the attacker did injure himself, his death is certain. But the time frame is vague."

"As far as I know, no one has questioned the major except me—and that was strictly routine. I think it's time we had a word. There'll be an outcry, of course, given his contacts with the security services."

"But if there's been a lack of cooperation . . ." Nan suggested.

"Right. What else can they expect?" He went to speak to the constable on duty and returned to say, "Ten minutes. Pack up your things, and I'll take you to the station. With a stop first at Larkin Manor."

Was I never going to see the end of country house visits? Apparently not. Carstairs had a plan. While he'd decided (correctly, I think) that I could not be considered a reliable witness, he thought Nan might recognize my attacker. Hence the stop at the manor where he planned to bring the major and my nan together. It was one of those plans that is better than nothing—but not much.

I was loaded into the backseat of Carstairs's car. Enveloped in stale tobacco smoke and bolstered by a couple of purloined hospital pillows and half a dozen towels, I lay holding my single crutch. Nan sat up front with Carstairs, turning around every few minutes to see how I was doing. Answer: not too well on the winding country roads. In fact, I was beginning to miss the curved metal pan that had sat beside my bed before we rolled up the long drive to the manor and parked out front.

I said that I needed some air, and though Nan looked concerned and Carstairs, irritated, they helped me out onto the gravel. I stuck my crutch under my arm and felt better for being upright. "You don't come in," said Carstairs. "Too obvious."

"Right." I waited until they went up to the front door then hobbled around the side of the house. I don't know why I had an impulse to look at the tower and the dig, especially when the horsey scent from the stable began to tickle my lungs, but I did. I hobbled down the path and skirted the dig—the dig that I will always feel mildly grateful for. I was about to return to the house before reaching rougher ground when I saw Jenkins standing in the shrubbery, a bottle in his hand.

I raised my hand but instead of calling hello, he placed a finger against his lips and signaled for me to approach. *A good idea, Francis?* I wasn't so sure, but the Agreeable One beckoned again and I limped across the lawn.

"Sorry," he said when I reached the shelter of the rhododendrons. "I don't want to be spotted from the house. Why are you here?"

"Inspector Carstairs brought me. We're on our way to London. He's looking for the major."

Jenkins was alarmed. "He mustn't find him. If he does, he'll want to take him into custody, to the hospital."

So it was true. My rascally uncle, who so often bends the truth to his own advantage, had been correct. "He tried to kill me," I said.

Jenkins nodded unhappily. "I knew nothing about that until it was too late. He was obsessed with the manor. He thought Inspector Davis and that Lastings chap were lying to him. He thought that he was under suspicion, that you knew about whatever Freddie had on him."

"We had nothing. At least nothing *I* knew of. He tried to stick me with something and hurt himself, instead."

"Yes. I drove him to Folkestone. He had a mad idea that he might recover at the seaside. Might as well have gone to Canterbury or Lourdes. As soon as he fell sick, he wanted to come back. He wants to die here."

"He's here?"

"He's hidden. He can't last. You needn't be afraid of him. But please don't tell the police or the madame."

Jenkins sounded sincere, but I've become suspicious. "I want to see him. I want to see for myself."

Jenkins shrugged uncomfortably. When he put his hand to his belt, I saw that he was armed with what looked like my uncle's Webley.

"Listen, if he is dying, I won't say anything. Not till he's gone. But if you shoot me, it's up instantly, isn't it?"

He hesitated only a moment, then took my arm. When we reached the dig wheelbarrow, he gestured toward it. I got awkwardly onto the barrow, which fortunately had a completely flat bed. Jenkins gave me the water bottle to hold, then seized the handles. We made our bumpy way around the stables toward the chapel. Of course, the last resting place of Larkin warriors. Jenkins helped me out at the side door. Inside, the low autumn light filtered through the plain yellowish modern glass and threw red, blue, and green patterns from the surviving stained windows. The place smelled of dusty stone and incense, and the only sounds were the calls of wood pigeons in the trees outside.

Jenkins gestured toward a heavy oak door off the main sanctuary. He tapped once on it, then unlocked it. The old chapel smell was swamped by the rotten smell of sickness, essence of hospital, such as I now recognized, minus the disinfectant overlay. The major lay on the floor on a pile of blankets, his head propped up on pillows. His face had gone all to bone, and the skin over the bones was thin and gray. Jenkins spoke to him without receiving an answer, and when he knelt down to check the major's pulse, he shook his head.

"I'm guessing massive organ failure," he said quietly. "He cannot last more than a few hours."

I heard the rattle and whistle of the major's breathing and thought even a few hours might be optimistic. "What was it? What sort of poison?"

"He said it was ricin, castor bean, but ultrarefined into an incredibly toxic pellet. Something the military had developed."

As if machine guns and poison gas hadn't proved deadly enough. The military mind has a great deal to answer for.

"He dies here," Jenkins said. "You must promise." And he touched the weapon stuck in his belt again.

It didn't take much imagination to see that there would be problems, complaints, and scandal if the major eluded the law. Not that I thought those legalities mattered, not when he was clearly dying from within. "All right. What about you? At the very least, you will be considered an accessory after the fact."

"Can I rely on you?" he asked. "When Major Larkin dies, I'll make a run for it. If you don't notify the police until tomorrow—tomorrow morning will surely be time enough—I'll be gone. That way the major will be found before his remains are too distressing."

When I nodded, he shook my hand. "Thank you, Francis. He saved my life when he got me out of the trenches. A lot of my mates were not so lucky."

The endless war. I could contribute nothing on that topic, and I didn't try. "Leave the door unlocked when you go," I said. "And wheel me as far as the stable. I'll manage from there."

Or so I thought. In the event, I barely made it back to Inspector Carstairs's car, and when I did, I was wheezing like a steam locomotive. Of course, Nan noticed that and also the earth on my trousers.

"I slipped looking at the dig. I didn't notice there was dew on the grass."

Nan clearly was dubious about that, but Carstairs was all in a sweat and didn't notice much of anything. The major had done a bunk. Off who knew where. And Jenkins, the footman, was missing as well. The car was in the garage. "Or," Carstairs said, simmering and quite near the boil, "the car had been in the garage. But now Thorne, I think he's the chauffeur, has been sent off on errands with it. Without as much as checking the mileage."

"I gather Mrs. Larkin was not much help."

"Mrs. Larkin could have fended off the Normans singlehandedly. Excuse me," he said to Nan.

"My feelings exactly," Nan said. She and Carstairs seemed

to be in complete agreement, and that was just as well, because by the time we reached the station, I was feeling woozy, and when Carstairs came to help me out of the back, he swore. I looked down; there was a large red patch on my trousers where the wound had started to bleed again.

Nan blamed it on my stumble at the dig. Carstairs, on the bad luck that dogged his professional life. He said I'd have to return to the hospital. Nan, however, opened her big black nanny's purse, a receptacle of useful items, and took out her scissors. She sacrificed my trouser leg, reinforced the leaking bandage with one of the hospital towels, and told Carstairs to take us to London. "Straight to the Royal London Hospital," she said. And he did.

CHAPTER 17

The next morning, Nan arrived at the hospital, where I had clean bandages and a new drain. My back was beginning to heal, and all I needed was the pair of trousers and the clean shirt that she had in a paper parcel. Plus, a fair sum of money to pay for my care.

"Dear boy," said Nan, dismissing these worries, "I have given them your uncle's name. He will submit a chit through the proper channels."

She'd sounded official enough to sway the medical staff, but I wasn't as easily convinced, especially since I had not yet confessed what I knew about Major Larkin. *No time like the present, Francis!* "We have to make a call to Inspector Carstairs," I said, and I described my encounter with Jenkins.

"You took a big risk, Francis." Nan's voice was unusually serious.

"Getting shot would have been worse. I felt I have enough perforations at the moment."

"Absolutely, you did the right thing! Except for wandering

from the car in the first place. But I think it best to get you home before I call. And what about contacting your uncle and that Inspector Davis?"

I thought a minute. "Let's give Carstairs an hour's head start."

"Perhaps via an anonymous tip? That way he can let the others know in his own good time and you can be kept out of it."

Never having to deal with Inspectors Davis or Carstairs or anyone at Larkin Manor ever again sounded too good to be true—and it was.

Although there was no proof that "the mystery woman caller" referred to in the press was Nan, Uncle Lastings carried on as if I'd endangered the realm, and Inspector Davis paid a visit to badger me about Jenkins. I professed complete ignorance, easy enough since I had no idea where the agreeable footman might have gone. I was delighted that he had gotten away, though, and I may have said that, too. *Not smart, Francis!*

Carstairs was the only member of officialdom who was happy with me. He had found the missing major, developed a plausible scenario for the Bosworth murder case, and turned over certain suspicious documents to "the proper authorities." Maybe we should have put his name on my hospital bill.

In between discussions with my unhappy uncle and various coppers, I returned to my design studio. I could work as long as my leg was elevated, and once I sorted through the scattered papers and drawings, I returned to fashionable chairs and avant-garde rugs. But though I finished up all the promised designs and saw that a number of commissioned rugs were delivered, my heart was no longer in quality furnishings. Nan said that I was recovering from shock and too impatient for my leg to heal.

I was certainly impatient, but I had no trouble working at my easel, even though the way I had to sit there made my leg ache. In fact, almost as soon as I got home, I'd begun a painting of the major as I'd seen him last, lying with all his bones visible and his flesh turning soft and melting into new forms. That's what I wanted to be working on, although I had difficulties with both the background and with the drawing despite some useful news photos.

When I told Maurice that I was wearied of chairs, he said, "Of course, Francis, there is nothing like the divine human form!"

Maurice was camping it up, but he was right. Even the things I'd enjoyed—the shiny metal frames of the chairs, the butter soft leather seats, the lovely rugs in their bold colors, the white rubber curtains that made the front window of my studio so distinctive—seemed insignificant, frivolous. Maybe that was it. Creating furniture for the rich and stylistically ambitious no longer seemed a good use of my time. Not when my time could be limited at any moment by tumbling from a high place or taking a toxic pellet.

But though I talked about making a change with both Nan and Maurice and spent time thinking about my future when I should have been working, I did not decide until the day Muriel visited. She came dressed for an afternoon party in a fox fur and a smart violet frock, and she wore a marvelous pair of purple heels that, with her upswept hair, brought her height past six feet. She carried a big bunch of flowers for Nan and a bottle of Champagne for me. "The chairs will be along presently," she said. "Ben's been so busy. There's been a bit of a change in the atmosphere lately, and business has been looking up."

"I'm glad of that," I said. "I'm just sorry I haven't yet been able to do anything for you." My uncle had made his displeasure clear and so had Davis. In their eyes, I was a loose cannon, incapable of following orders (not that mine had been particularly explicit!), and they'd been so angry that I'd been afraid to ask about the Mendelssohns. Thinking that time, as Nan says, is the great healer, I'd postponed the subject.

"I don't know what you mean by anything," Muriel said. "Unless you expected the palace to send an equerry in a coach and four for the delivery."

When she saw my surprise, she pulled out a British passport with the golden lion and unicorn seal made out to *Mrs. M. Mendelssohn.* "How's that?"

"Marvelous!" I said and gave her a congratulatory kiss. "But what about Ben? Did Ben get one, too?"

"He certainly did, and His Majesty will not have a more faithful and enthusiastic subject anywhere."

I called through to Nan, who was fixing her flowers in the kitchen. "Let's open that Champagne! We need to celebrate."

Nan brought a tray with glasses and slices of her tea cake with raisins and candied cherries, and we poured the Champagne and had what she calls a "good gossip." First, about the Mendelssohns' passports, the anxiety before and the joy afterward, and the interesting hints along the way of "official interest."

"Damn right!" I said and thought gratefully of Miss Fallowfield and Mac.

Then we moved on to my carefully edited adventures in darkest Sussex before reaching Poppy, who I guess we must say was the initial cause of everything.

"She hasn't been to see Francis," Nan said. This was a huge black mark against my cousin.

"Oh, she's not in London," Muriel said. "I saw her just before she left. She's gotten the theatrical bug and gone off with a small troupe. They have a very handsome leading man." She raised her eyebrows. "The sins of one's youth."

"He'll almost certainly be safer than Freddie Bosworth."

"Maybe. But I gather that it is the travel that really attracts her."

"Where might they be going?" Nan asked. "The Midlands and the north?"

"A bit more glamorous, supposedly." Muriel frowned with distaste. "Germany, Austria, northern Italy. The fascist circuit. Not where I'd set foot. But she was excited about the prospect. *Actors can go anywhere and their dressers go with them.* That's what she said. I tried to tell her that the life of the stage gypsy gets old after a while."

"But it kept you young," I said.

Muriel laughed and patted my knee. "Flattery, flattery. But we are truly grateful, Francis. I never made a better thing out of loaning a dress! And you will get your chairs soon."

In that moment, I made up my mind. "Keep the chairs for your new apartment. No charge. I've decided to break up the design studio. It's run its course, and I'm going to take a stab at painting."

"Serious artistic ambition!" exclaimed Muriel. "No more chorus, straight to the spotlight. Best of luck."

"We must have another glass for luck," said Nan, who is fond of good Champagne.

"You're sure you don't mind?" I asked. "I'm afraid we'll be poor."

"I've been poor," she said in a reflective tone. "Money's better, but life's too short to pass on happiness."

"Amen to that," said Muriel. "To the arts, a blessing and a curse! And I'll have another slice of that cake, since I don't have to weigh in anymore."

We raised our glasses, and I felt the best I'd been since my fall from the tower. It was a jolly party, but after Muriel left, I got serious with Nan. I poured out the last drops of Champagne and asked, "Are you sure you don't have doubts about this? I'll have to find work of some sort as a backup. Whatever I get will probably be steadier but not as profitable as the design studio."

"We'll manage," she said stoutly. "There must be cranky old ladies in London who need companions."

"No," I said. "No more of that for you. See to the housekeeping and I'll see to the cash."

"Dear boy." She raised her glass and touched it to mine. "You know, Francis," she said after a moment, "the only thing I have doubts about is your cousin."

"Poppy?"

She nodded. "Dressers work hard. They need to be able to sew well, too. Something Miss Penelope never learned. And they don't keep horses. That's her real love."

"Yes, but the theatrical life may be an easier way to annoy

her mother than getting engaged to the Freddie Bosworths of this world."

"I was wondering," Nan said carefully, "if that engagement was less about annoying her mother and more about keeping an eye on Bosworth."

Talk about a different perspective! One that opened avenues that I wasn't sure I liked at all.

"Her father was in military intelligence," Nan continued. "Your cousin adored him. Not that she knew him terribly well or saw too much of him, you understand, but that is often grounds for adoration."

I certainly could have liked my father more with greater distance and less frequency.

"Then there's her uncle—your uncle Lastings. And their old family friend, Major Larkin." Nan pronounced his name with real distaste. "They are all more or less in the spy business or have been. Do you see what I am saying?"

"I do."

"And now she's off on— What did you friend Muriel call it?"

"The fascist circuit."

"She's an intelligent young woman," Nan said, "yet she's gone off with a third-rate troupe into dodgy territory."

"The leading man is handsome. And Poppy thought well of Mussolini. Or said she did."

"She'd have to, wouldn't she?" Nan observed. "But it was just an idle thought, dear boy. I don't think you have to worry. I'm sure you'll make a go of painting, and I think Miss Penelope knows how to take care of herself."

I certainly agreed with the latter, and between nursing my leg and winding up Avant Design, I didn't think too much about my cousin or her mysterious journey until several weeks later.

I was drain free and unbandaged with only a few lingering scabs to show that I had been in a horticultural embrace. The design business was closed, and we'd obtained new digs with a good-size painting studio for me. I was crossing Soho Square on some last-minute errands when a familiar voice said, "I do believe that's Francis."

My initial impulse was to close my ears and keep on walking. But if Uncle Lastings is often inconvenient, he's always interesting. I turned around and momentarily thought that my ears had deceived me: There was an apparition in a pin-striped dark navy suit with a handsome tie and expensive shoes. His hair, which had been growing out from red after his foray as a Frenchman, was now a fine shade of platinum. My uncle looked like money and influence, and my immediate thought was that he'd pulled off another outrageous scam.

"Quite recovered?" he asked.

I should mention that after our unpleasant conversation about the major, I hadn't had a word from him. So much for family feeling!

"Quite. You look to be thriving yourself."

He automatically touched his regimental tie. "My services have been recognized, my boy, with a consular post. A minor position," he added modestly, "but one in a splendid climate."

Will wonders never cease? "Congratulations," I said, "The Foreign Office is certainly growing broad-minded."

"Do I detect a note of bitterness? Allow me to buy you lunch. What about Quo Vadis?"

The proprietor was a big Mussolini man, but his clientele ranged the political spectrum. "If you're picking up the check."

"Indeed I am. Just as I picked up the bills for your recent hospital stay."

"His Majesty's government certainly owed me that!"

My uncle sniffed and rolled his eyes. "Agreed. I was perhaps a little harsh at our last meeting, Francis. It was a delicate matter all around. However, Larkin's autopsy showed that you were quite correct: The poor major would have been in no shape for questioning even had you raised the alarm. Pity, but there it was."

I nodded.

"It was felt best to remember his sterling war service to king and country and to pass over any connection with the murder of a man who was definitely a blackmailer and probably a traitor."

He already sounded like a bureaucrat. "Generously high-minded, if ignoring the fact that he nearly murdered me, too."

"He was a bit unhinged at the end," said my uncle. "But you know, Francis, the military mind is rarely at ease with improvisation and eccentricity in the line of duty."

"I hope you are not claiming that I provoked the major's attack."

"No," said Uncle Lastings without sounding convinced. "It was not up to me. I would naturally have taken a different tack, but the higher powers refused to proceed. Given that your usefulness was at an end."

I felt myself becoming irked. "And what about Poppy? Is she still useful?"

I got a close sharp look.

"I think you might have left her out of this," I added.

"That's where you're wrong. Your cousin Penelope has the family's fighting spirit. Males in our line being in short supply—"

"Or endowed with common sense."

"—there was interest when she offered her talents."

"She was involved from the first, then?"

"No, not at all. I gather that she only gradually became suspicious of Freddie and his friends. Quite naturally, she consulted Major Larkin."

"Hence that awkward country house party."

He nodded.

"Which offered the major an unexpected chance to eliminate the man who'd been blackmailing him?"

"That's the assumption, though proof is in short supply. We'd rather Bosworth had been spared, to tell you the truth. But Tollman and Grove and Armitage were a decent bag, along with enough evidence to force Signor Rinaldi's recall."

"For which you've taken most of the credit," I said.

"Certainly, my boy. What would you do with a consular post in the tropics but die of boredom? You have splendid talents, Francis, but they do not run to anything bureaucratic."

"You got me into hot water just the same."

"With good results, though. Now that Muriel Mendelssohn—what a physique! A noble woman! You'd given me no idea of her charm." I got a resentful look as though a heads-up from me could have secured his happiness.

"I owed her," I said.

"Well, now, you've been able to pay your debt. So, Francis, for old times' sake? Lunch with Champagne?"

I only hesitated for a minute. "If you promise never to call on me again."

"I wouldn't think of it," said my uncle. "I intend to move in very different circles from now on."

Good luck to the Foreign Office, I thought, and as he started to elaborate on future plans, I thought it wise to take his arm lest rhetoric carry him away.

ABOUT THE AUTHOR

Janice Law is an acclaimed author of mystery fiction. The Watergate scandal inspired her to write her first novel, *The Big Payoff*, which introduced Anna Peters, a street-smart young woman who blackmails her boss, a corrupt oil executive. The novel was a success, winning an Edgar nomination, and Law went on to write eight more in the series. Law has written historical mysteries, standalone suspense, and, most recently, the Francis Bacon Mysteries, which include *The Prisoner of the Riviera*, winner of the 2013 Lambda Literary Gay Mystery Award. She lives and writes in Connecticut.

THE FRANCIS BACON MYSTERIES

FROM MYSTERIOUSPRESS.COM
AND OPEN ROAD MEDIA

MYSTERIOUSPRESS.COM

OPEN ROAD
INTEGRATED MEDIA

MYSTERIOUSPRESS.COM

Otto Penzler, owner of the Mysterious Bookshop in Manhattan, founded the Mysterious Press in 1975. Penzler quickly became known for his outstanding selection of mystery, crime, and suspense books, both from his imprint and in his store. The imprint was devoted to printing the best books in these genres, using fine paper and top dust-jacket artists, as well as offering many limited, signed editions.

Now the Mysterious Press has gone digital, publishing ebooks through **MysteriousPress.com**.

MysteriousPress.com offers readers essential noir and suspense fiction, hard-boiled crime novels, and the latest thrillers from both debut authors and mystery masters. Discover classics and new voices, all from one legendary source.

FIND OUT MORE AT

WWW.MYSTERIOUSPRESS.COM

FOLLOW US:

@emysteries and Facebook.com/MysteriousPressCom

MysteriousPress.com is one of a select group of publishing partners of Open Road Integrated Media, Inc.

THE MYSTERIOUS BOOKSHOP, founded in 1979, is located in Manhattan's Tribeca neighborhood. It is the oldest and largest mystery-specialty bookstore in America.

The shop stocks the finest selection of new mystery hardcovers, paperbacks, and periodicals. It also features a superb collection of signed modern first editions, rare and collectable works, and Sherlock Holmes titles. The bookshop issues a free monthly newsletter highlighting its book clubs, new releases, events, and recently acquired books.

58 Warren Street
info@mysteriousbookshop.com
(212) 587-1011
Monday through Saturday
11:00 a.m. to 7:00 p.m.

FIND OUT MORE AT:

www.mysteriousbookshop.com

FOLLOW US:

@TheMysterious and Facebook.com/MysteriousBookshop

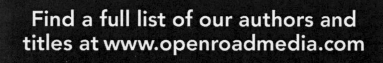

CPSIA information can be obtained
at www.ICGtesting.com
Printed in the USA
FFOW03n2014131017
40980FF